# PRAIS

"Leave it to Zibby Owens to write a novel about a lovable woman single-handedly disrupting the publishing industry. *Blank* explores marriage, parenting, friendship, and the competitive high jinks of the book trade with the perfect amount of wit and light-touch humor. I devoured this book in a single sitting."

—Annabel Monaghan, author of *Nora Goes Off Script* and *Same Time Next Summer*

"This is a sunny rom-com with a deep, dark heart—comedic and sad in equal measures. Yes, it's a meta-satire about the publishing industry, but it's also an authentically serious story about the pressure to be everything to everyone. Or, in other words, about what it means to be a woman."

—Catherine Newman, author of *We All Want Impossible Things*

"Zibby Owens captures every writer's nightmare in her fiction debut: someone beats you to the bookshelves with basically the same book you are currently writing. Add to this some genuine home drama, financial worries, and trouble in paradise, and you have a book that you race through because you just want to know what is going to happen!"

—Laurie Gelman, author of the Class Mom series

"Is there anything literary North Star Zibby Owens can't do? Add novelist to her list of breaking-down-the-barriers accomplishments, and here, in this smart, hilarious, ingenious, and absolutely inspiring novel, Owens ebulliently cracks open marriage, motherhood, female friendship, social media, the perils of publishing—and our yearning to be seen, loved and understood. I was turning pages so fast, I nearly gave myself whiplash."

—Caroline Leavitt, *New York Times* bestselling author of *Pictures of You* and *With or Without You*

"A witty romp, *Blank* is the perfect addition to book lovers' bedside tables. An insider's view of the publishing industry and a wise and beautiful celebration of love, *Blank* kept me happily reading all night and left me bereft when I reached the end of my journey with Owens's wise and fabulous heroine Pippa."

—Amanda Eyre Ward, author of *The Lifeguards* and *The Jetsetters*

"A delectable, engaging romp through the upper crust of the LA and New York literary worlds but refreshingly grounded and relatable, *Blank* is like sharing a cool glass of pinot gris with Zibby on a hot day, which is to say: a total treat."

—Bess Kalb, author of *Nobody Will Tell You This But Me*

"*Blank* is full of wit, verve, and heart—a whirlwind ride with a heroine you can't help rooting for. Readers will laugh, wince, and cheer as Pippa writes the next (blank?) chapter of her career, navigates the pain of betrayal, and seizes the happiness she deserves."

—Jane Roper, author of *The Society of Shame*

"Zibby Owens is a tremendous champion for writers, and it's thrilling to see her own storytelling shine in this smart debut novel about marriage, motherhood, and finding your purpose. *Blank* is a romp through the publishing world and a delightful gift to book lovers."

—Carley Fortune, #1 New York Times bestselling author of *Meet Me at the Lake* and *Every Summer After*

"I read it in one sitting, and loved it. *Blank* has Zibby's inimitable voice, of course, and she also has told a story which feels like a parable not only of her own story, in ways, but of publishing, which is to say a novel that dovetails with the movement she herself has built, inspiring women to tell their stories, inspiring authors to tear down old walls."

—Lea Carpenter, author of *Ilium*, *Eleven Days*, and *Red, White, Blue*

BLANK

# BLANK

A NOVEL

## ZIBBY OWENS

Little
a

Text copyright © 2024 by Zibby Owens
All rights reserved.

Published by Little A, New York

www.apub.com

Amazon, the Amazon logo, and Little A are trademarks of Amazon.com, Inc., or its affiliates.

ISBN-13: 9781662516696 (hardcover)
ISBN-13: 9781662516702 (paperback)
ISBN-13: 9781662511196 (digital)

Cover design by Tree Abraham

Printed in the United States of America

First edition

*To Max. Next time I'll have the chocolate chip pancakes ready.*

*—Mom, aka Pippa Jones*


*To G. C. R. Next time I'll have the chocolate chip pancakes ready.*

*—Mom, aka Zibby Owens*

# MONDAY

# One

"Mom, look!"

"Zoe? Are you okay?"

It was the middle of the night and I'd just woken up to a cellphone being shoved in front of my face. Great. Now I'd never fall back asleep. Well, at least I could start writing early.

"I told you they were getting together! See? I knew he didn't like me."

"What time is it?" I struggled to sit up in the dark.

"Look! See his hand on her back?"

"Whose hand?"

"Just look!"

I fumbled for and grabbed my reading glasses off the stack of books on my bedside table, slid them on, and looked at the Instagram post of two canoodling teens. When the kids were little, I was sure my sleepless nights would soon be over for good. Not a chance. At age fifteen, Zoe still seemed to have no grasp of the distinction between night and day and the fact that other people needed to sleep. Or maybe she just didn't care? Plus, now that they could sleep, I couldn't. Aging is so much fun.

"Okay, fine. Yes. It looks like they're together."

She gasped.

"It looks like they're *together*?"

"Yes, isn't that what you wanted me to say?"

"NO! I wanted you to tell me I was being crazy, that Todd was still into *me*."

I sighed, tossed my glasses on the books, and fell back on my pillow.

"I can't win. Why even ask me? I think I told my mother about literally *one* boy I liked at your age."

"Well, I wouldn't tell Gee-Gee anything either."

My mother, Joan, was a character, deeply consumed with her own *mishigas*. She was perpetually clad in Palm Springs mid-century-modern caftans, ice clinking in a lowball glass as she wandered from room to room. Her two chihuahuas were always scampering after her, my stepfather, Seymour, not too far behind.

"Could the two of you just be quiet," Ethan groaned. "Zoe, no one's ever going to like you and you'll die alone. Is that what you want us to say?"

I pretend-smacked Ethan. Perhaps a little too hard.

"Ouch!"

"Da-aaad!"

"Zoe, he's kidding. But go back to bed. Please. Get some rest, sweetie. You have school tomorrow."

"Fine, but I'm commenting on this post so the two of them know I know."

"Look, if this guy Todd isn't into you, he's a moron," Ethan said. "You should just move on. His loss."

Now that my eyes had adjusted to the dark, I could see Zoe stomping out in her favorite tie-dye T-shirt and influencer-famous joggers, twisting her long, stick-straight light-brown hair into a messy bun. Usually she wore giant sweatshirts (all styles were inexplicably referred to as "hoodies") to hide her petite, athletic body. The swooshing sounds of outgoing text messages trailed her down the hallway.

"We should take that phone away," Ethan mumbled.

"Mmm," I said, pulling the covers back up. "You're right."

Ethan rolled over and was snoring again within seconds. *How is that even physically possible?* I glanced over and saw the top of his familiar, faded blue-and-white-striped jammies, worn almost translucent over the years. He refused to replace them. Why waste money?

His formerly thick, wavy brown hair was now infused with a few shocks of gray and was thinning, not that we could ever acknowledge it to each other. I just kept sweeping the hairs off the bathroom floor, the pillows, even the toilet seat. After seventeen years together, I knew which "buttons" of his to avoid pushing. His blue eyes, now closed, were paired with seriously long and highly enviable eyelashes that our son, Max, had inherited—along with his dimples. Not that Ethan had smiled much lately.

I sighed deeply, my eyes open like a cat in the nighttime even though I knew I should be sleeping. *I knew it;* I was wide awake and it was only 3:14 a.m. I scanned the ceiling for cracks as I went back to worrying about my book.

My novel was three *years* overdue. *Years!* How could I possibly follow up *Poppies* with something I was proud of? *Poppies*, my debut novel about an heiress forced to navigate the 2008 housing crisis by selling all her Hermès purses and uniting a tribe of underutilized women, had been an unexpected bestseller. And then it was made into a film and won an Academy Award. For best sound mixing, yes, but whatever. *Poppies* had become a cult hit among a certain social set, and in Hollywood currency, I'd made it.

"A slam dunk from a debut author," claimed *Vanity Fair.* "Pippa Jones is the voice of a generation!"

Sales sped along, women toting their Birkins to readings, tittering about the plot in their book clubs for which they'd each bought two copies because *why not?* It was enough for my book to earn out its admittedly meager advance and start paying me "royalties," a few cents for every book sold, which really added up. It added up enough, that is, for me to finally pay for highlights instead of dipping into Ethan's savings from his career as a child actor, a rapidly draining pot. (Ethan had told me long ago that "his wife going gray" wasn't something he'd be "cool" with, despite the dwindling strands atop his head.)

My longtime literary agent, LeeLee, had been thrilled by the success of *Poppies*. At least I *think* she was thrilled. Her face didn't move that much with all the fillers. When she smiled, she looked like some sort of frozen fish trying to escape from a net. A blonde net. Not that it mattered, because I almost never saw her in person. She definitely *sounded* happy when she called from her vintage Saab to tell me *Poppies* had hit the *New York Times* bestseller list ("the list"). But my bespectacled, tattooed New York editor, Sidonie, had been truly over the moon from day one. She'd dreamed of it being optioned and made into a movie starring one-named celebrities I'd never heard of.

"*Sireneuse! Mayhew! Persephone!*"

*May-who?!* When did everyone get so young and famous? Sidonie and her wife, the Australian guitarist Jade, had sat in the front row of the premiere.

Naturally.

But now the dust had settled. After the movie left theaters, my publisher, Driftwood, basically forgot about me. One of their other titles had been chosen as a big book club pick, and the third book from one of their beloved thriller authors was coming out. Yes, my hit was great. But it was a single; I hadn't proven myself with a home run yet. And, apparently, it wasn't enough to keep their eyes on me.

But that's what happens in publishing. Today's darling quickly becomes tomorrow's doorstop. And those authors whose books came out and barely sold? Forget it. Of course, many of those overlooked books are amazing. Spectacular, even. Like a lost child at a crowded festival, a debut novelist could simply disappear, blending in with the background. It wasn't fair. It wasn't fair that talent didn't equate success, that some wildly popular authors weren't the best at their craft, whereas some gifted novelists sold, like, two copies of their book. To their parents.

*Poppies* disappeared from the list like a one-night stand slinking out the door the next morning, still buckling his belt. The fireworks had dissolved into mere clouds of smoke. All the excited emails from Brittany, my publicist, had stopped coming in except for a few errant newbie podcasters tossing their hats in the PR ring.

"Never say no!" Brittany advised.

Nobody cared about *Poppies*, or me, anymore. They were on to the next big thing. *Hot summer reads! Lily Opum's new novel! The film adaptation of* The Grasshopper*!* I was yesterday's news. Not even. Like, last decade's news. Unless I could write myself back into the narrative, I was destined to be a one-hit wonder. I wouldn't have minded as much if we had, well, everlasting financial security. But with Ethan's theater producer job not exactly bringing in the big bucks—there are, like, three plays a *year* in LA—and with my writing stalling, it was tough paying two private-school tuitions and everything else. I mean, I guess I didn't *have* to send them to private school. The advance on my new book from three years ago? Poof. I'd used it to turn the kitchen pantry into my writing office.

Thanks to Ethan's residual income, we could lead our very privileged upper-middle-class life, but we were toeing the line constantly, spending heavily on all the trappings seemingly required of it (Summer camp! School auction! Vacations!) that hit us hard. We didn't have endless reserves like many of our peers, and despite how fortunate we were, there was always an undercurrent of tension. My writing income helped, but one book wouldn't cut it to maintain this lifestyle forever. When would it run out? And what then?

I turned onto my side and curled into a ball, my arms hugging my knees to my chest. My eyes were wide open like I'd just had a jolt of epinephrine. Should I read? And, wait, what was that on Ethan's pillow? I inched closer to his side, propped myself up on my elbow, and examined the many hairs that had taken up residence on his pillow. The hair loss must be killing him. And yet he was plenty happy weighing in on my hair color. Really. The nerve! Honestly, I didn't care. I just didn't love the whole double standard thing. And yes. Those were his hairs alright. He looked so sweet when he was asleep. If only it would stay that way.

Tossing and turning wasn't helping anything. I was just getting more anxious.

Okay, time for a quick Instagram check. What was everyone else up to? And how was my account doing? Or rather, accounts. I imagined throngs of women my age underneath the covers in the dead of night, scrolling mindlessly. Many of us used to be up at this hour nursing, comforting crying kids, depositing errant dollar bills as tooth fairies. Now we were all awake, our kids out cold in messy rooms down the hall, our minds spinning, hormones toying with us. "Oh yeah? You think you can sleep *now*?" they taunted.

I'd started doing something else, something secret, salacious, and totally time-consuming. I'd launched an underground Instagram account documenting the hidden parts of luxurious houses on the market in LA. *That* kind of writing I could do easily. Captions! Pithy! Fun!

Like Ruth Reichl was for restaurants—anonymously dining in disguise to review the latest hot spots—I was the undercover real estate whisperer. If there was an open house in the LA area, I was there. Taking pictures. Posting. Adding funny comments. Real estate brokers often joked about "me." I'd even been called out on the hit reality show *Brentwood Brokers*. One real estate agent said to the other, "I hope @openhousebandit doesn't strike again. I *need* people to love my new listing!"

I'd watched that episode on the couch next to Ethan, who was busy on his phone the whole time, and exclaimed, "No WAY!" pitching forward to get closer to the screen.

"What?" Ethan had asked, not looking up.

"Nothing, nothing," I'd said, sinking back. But it was amazing. I just smiled to myself and kept watching, pulling the cozy cream chenille blanket on top of me. If only I could monetize *that* without revealing my identity.

For whatever reason, I loved sneaking into strangers' homes, trying to figure out their stories. My old therapist would've had a field day with that: searching for a home given my own fractured family.

But boy, was I a sucker for wallpaper. Turned out I wasn't the only one obsessed. My 710K followers watched my every move. I didn't tell *anyone* it was me. Not Ethan, not my kids. Not even Kelly, Gabriela, and Josie, my three best friends from college. We still talked all the time and got together once a month for virtual book club. It was the only thing that made me feel like *me* when every other part of me was wrapped up in being a wife, mom, daughter, nonwriting author, and former big deal. Who else *was* I? Apparently, a witty luxury-home connoisseur who could spot a four-bedroom with space for a powder room from a mile away.

# Two

B link. Blink, blink.

Have you ever *really* thought about the cursor? I texted Kelly. Why does it have to blink like that?

Three dots.

Oh boy. That kind of writing day?

Can't you just hear horror music playing in the background as it slowly tolls the death knell?

The 5:00 a.m. writing session had not gone well. Of course, I hadn't been able to fall back asleep. I'd stood at the Keurig, watching the drips of my creative fuel plop into my favorite mug with the *Moms Don't Have Time to Read Books* podcast logo. So true! Moms don't even have time to read school emails let alone entire books. Although I tried to always read our book club pick.

Gripping the ceramic mug with two hands, bypassing the handle, I put on my writing slippers—one said "Don't," the other said "Trip"—pulled up the hood of my favorite blue sweatshirt, and shuffled to my desk. Then, I opened the top drawer and pulled out one of the forty-seven single-serving packets of chocolate-covered almonds I'd stockpiled from Starbucks (they were hard to find, so I splurged when they were in stock) and sat down on my yellow upholstered chair, wheeling it up to the computer. I closed out of all tabs so nothing would distract me and opened the Word document. Then I took a deep breath, perched my fingers over the keys like a pianist about to pounce, and then . . . nothing.

Another text came in from Kelly on the East Coast.

You need sleep.

True.

My new "office" off the kitchen was a mishmash of books, magazines, bills, boxes, and discarded coffee mugs. I anxiously started texting back.

It's like a ticking time bomb. A heartbeat.

Just stop, Kelly replied. Face the fear. Just get in the document.

Easy for you to say, I wrote back. Miss I'm-on-page-367-of-my-57th-thriller.

F off.

Kelly, Gabriela, Josie, and I had found each other in the school newspaper office freshman year at Bluestone University. We'd *all* wanted to be writers back then. Surrounded by stacks of yellowing papers, racks of leather-bound books, and even a few old typewriters, we were the only women among a sea of wannabe Woodwards and Bernsteins.

"So, you all think you're gonna be journalists?" said Alex, the preppy senior and managing editor of the *Bluesheet*. "By the end of the day, half of you will have rethought your decision."

*Huh? What is this?!*

I'd quickly glanced at the three girls, catching the eye of the brunette on my left. She shrugged, then began taking down notes.

"Your assignment," Alex went on, walking in slow circles around us seated newbies, "is to break a story about a building on campus. Find the hidden meaning. The secrets. The *lies*."

He bent down and looked a tall Black girl in the eye.

"All of it."

She leaned back as far as possible in her chair. Then she looked over at us, her eyes wide. Gorgeous and almost six feet tall, she didn't seem easily intimidated.

"Put a thousand words of copy on my desk, printed, by nine a.m. tomorrow. Good luck." Alex stood, hands on hips, nodding. "You'll need it," he said, chuckling to himself. Then he tucked his white polo shirt tighter into his Nantucket reds and retreated back into the newsroom.

I'd looked at the three other women, all of us stunned into silence, and said, "The glee club is sounding pretty good right about now."

We all stood up and introduced ourselves.

"I'm Kelly, from New York." Kelly had straight, thin, shoulder-length, white-blonde hair; a trace of freckles; superlong eyelashes; and a narrow face with a tight smile. At five foot two, her body was lean and tiny. Yet tough. Although her parents had pushed her to be a ballerina or a figure skater, Kelly had been drawn to martial arts and fallen for the far-less-feminine jujitsu. She'd never forgiven her parents for forbidding her from going to the regional competitions; she knew she could have crushed them.

The Black girl waved to our circle with a little knee bend and a smile.

"Josie. Chicago. Nice to meet you."

Josie's hair was pulled back in a bun, and her smooth tawny skin offset dark, soulful, shining eyes set a tad farther apart than expected. She could have been a model—her limbs flowing, her posture perfectly upright, whereas I was always slumped over. She'd found her calling in ballet and then modern dance, dressed in black unitards with cat's-eye makeup, moving melodiously through various poses to percussive, gong-filled music. Her observational nature and comfort with her body drew her to other cultural outlets, and before she knew it, she'd become the Arts & Culture editor of her high school newspaper and even had a radio show with a classmate discussing politics and current events with her astute, brilliant remarks. It was no huge shock when, after earning her stripes at every local news network in the US years later, she eventually became a renowned correspondent. Single. Stunning but not aware of it. Accomplished.

"I'm Gabriela. From Venezuela." Gabriela looked like an athlete; her black tank top accentuated her broad shoulders, narrow waist, and toned biceps. I'd later learn that she was overweight as a child until she discovered all types of sports—especially competitive swimming, for which she'd been recruited to Bluestone. She was striking looking, like Anjelica Huston, with very full lips, a narrow nose, and dark-brown hair with bangs. But it was her fabulous sense of humor that had always attracted everyone to her side of the room.

And me?

I preferred to be called "a natural beauty," not that anyone was really calling me that. I was a bit mousy. Pale despite the constant sunshine in my hometown of LA. A quick wit, yes, but a nondescript outer edge. I often looked like what my mother classified as "not making an effort." I was usually in jeans, a T-shirt, and flip-flops. I had an Ashkenazi vibe, with an oval face, high cheekbones, lips that didn't require lipstick, a normal-size nose, and some errant beauty marks that I had debated getting removed. I typically had a chipped manicure or none at all and wavy (read: frizzy) hair that attracted humidity like a barometer and required a superpowered hair dryer. And yet somehow it all worked together.

"Hi, ladies. I'm Pippa. I'm from LA," I said, smiling. "Anyone ready to hunt for some secrets?"

"Um, not me," Josie answered.

"Same," Kelly added.

"Forget this assignment! Seriously. What was *with* that guy?!" said Gabriela. "How about we head to a bookstore and grab some coffee instead?"

We all walked straight to the Bluestone Coop and browsed the aisles together. I stood, feet planted, in the memoir section. Josie read every hardcover flap in the history and biography area. Kelly browsed the thrillers, while Gabriela checked out the Spanish-language section. We all loved books more than anything, certainly more than any of the boys we would meet over the next four years.

We'd been through a lot together since those early days. Boyfriends. Weddings. Kids. Job changes. Josie's mom's car accident. Kelly's dad's lung cancer scare. Gabriela's affairs. Family dramas. Grad schools.

Life.

Kelly didn't give up on journalism that day, though. She'd go on to found *Hi-YA!*, now the world's leading martial arts magazine, and then sell it to Condé Nast. She met her husband, Arthur, a sumo wrestler turned finance whiz, when she interviewed him for a piece on weight-gain hacks and fell deeply in love. They ended up with three perfectly coiffed, towheaded, tae-kwon-do-champion, private-school kids in New York and a membership at the exclusive country club in Southampton that her father and grandfather had belonged to.

She left the print media world after her magazine was acquired, only to start whipping out mind-bending, twisty, coveted reads set in the martial arts world. The novels focused on the various forms, from karate to Krav Maga; she sold them at tournaments until a few postings on popular martial arts handles made them go viral. For the last twelve years, every single one had been a bestseller. And yes, I kind of hated her for it. Not that I would ever admit it. Her husband had dropped three hundred pounds on Atkins, gone to business school, and become a hedge fund guru as founder of Sumo Capital. They were fixtures in the charity circuit, always the most interesting dinner party conversationalists.

I didn't know how Kelly did it all. Holiday cards that arrived the day after Thanksgiving with a photo of her identically dressed kids, shelves of trophies behind them. Thoughtful flowers that showed up on my birthday each year. Elegantly wrapped presents for all the kids' big days. (I could barely remember my own kids' birthdays, let alone someone else's. And holiday cards? Late or never.) And in her spare time, Kelly played the flute. I mean, *come on.*

Look, Kelly texted, just write what you know. Don't be so precious about it. Write about me! Gabriela! Josie. Our book club. Whatever. Just get into the document.

Okay, okay, I texted back. Thanks.

We sent each other heart emojis. Maybe I could write about heart emojis? *How to make that interesting . . .* Maybe what happens when someone sends the wrong person a salacious emoji? I spent the early-morning hours writing scene after scene, pausing only to get a fresh cup of coffee. And then, right before waking up the kids, I read it all back. It was terrible. Unsalvageable. Embarrassing.

Select all.

Delete.

Moms don't have time to write terrible drafts.

Wasted morning writing. Don't even ask, I texted Kelly as I walked upstairs to wake the kids. What were we supposed to read for book club again tonight? I'm pretty sure I read it, but now I forget. I swear I'm losing my mind.

No writing is a waste! And the book assignments are in the Google Doc.

My Google Docs disappear, I wrote back. For some reason I can never find them again after opening them once. Where do they go?! I should write a book called The Mysterious Disappearance of the Google Doc.

We're reading Writers & Lovers by Lily King. And no, you should not write that book. Have to run. The kids are making egg white omelets for breakfast and I promised I'd watch. Check the Google Drive!

Her kids were making omelets. Meanwhile my kids needed me to pour Honey Nut Cheerios in a bowl for them.

I sighed deeply and texted again: Google Drive is even worse than Google Docs. Maybe my Google Drive got into a car accident. It got lost. It got its driver's license revoked.

Okay, you have to stop. Not funny.

I laughed.

Love you.

# Three

"Time to get up! Guys? Wakey, wakey! It's already time to leave!"
I was standing at the top of the bleached-wood stairs, admiring the blue-and-white sisal runner from Overstock while rousing Zoe and Max. They were going to be late for school. Again.

"Seriously. Guys! Come on!" I knocked on both their doors.

Zoe opened hers and gave me a quick hug; she basically just hugged my left shoulder. Pink hair extensions were braided through her long locks, which she'd swept into a high pony. A black crop top left her waist exposed, her belly button peeking out above her jeans, finished off with an open oversize hoodie and Air Force Ones.

"You can't say 'guys' anymore," she said, and headed downstairs, stomping so loudly I thought the wood might crack.

"What? Seriously?"

Max came running out of his room. Small for his age, he seemed to be half the size of his backpack. He hunched over from the weight of it.

"Hi, love," I said as he gave me a quick kiss on the cheek. "Is that true? I'm not supposed to say 'guys' anymore?"

He shrugged.

"No one tells me anything," he answered, his just pubescent voice cracking a bit as he rubbed the sleep from his eyes.

We headed downstairs together to find Zoe in the kitchen staring at her phone. "Let's grab a quick breakfast for the road. We're late. What do you two want?"

No one answered. As I opened the fridge to grab some yogurt pouches, I glanced around the room. I *loved* our kitchen. Open glass cabinets with plain white CB2 plates and mugs. Forest-green cabinets. A beautiful green-and-brown jaguar-print wallpaper as an accent on one wall. A huge island with three sturdy wood and leather stools. Sunlight pouring in through the skylight.

*A+ kitchen with natural light, ample storage, a dishwasher, two sinks, and a six-burner range.* It was our home's main selling point when I'd scanned the listing. And the Pacific Palisades location couldn't be beat; the ocean was only ten minutes away. Ethan's residual income from reruns of his show backed the mortgage we'd taken out. I stepped into the flip-flops I'd left by the door; grabbed a banana, my sunglasses, and the car keys; and headed out with the kids following me, barely looking up from their phones.

"You know, Mom, it's really not good to eat on the go. We're all supposed to sit down and be mindful of what we're eating," Zoe said. *Classic.* One minute she was waking me up in a panic about the doomed state of her love life; the next she was lecturing me on proper eating habits. *Oh, the joys of parenting a teenager.*

"Yes, I know that, love. Thank you," I said. "But sometimes *not* being perfect is okay, too. And could you maybe get off your phone for two minutes, please? If you hadn't overslept, we might have had time for a proper meal."

"I'm just texting Greta. And whatever. You could've woken me up earlier. What, were you writing all morning again?"

Max looked up from his phone as he zombie-walked.

"Can I have chocolate chip pancakes?"

"Max, there's no time. We're *literally* walking out," I said, motioning to the back door and the lush California greenery.

"A big dose of carbs first thing in the morning is *really* bad for you," Zoe started. "Protein is a better—"

"Zoe! Enough. Just get in the car. We're going to be late. Save the nutrition lecture for the backseat."

"But—"

"ZOE! Car!"

"Okay, okay," she said.

"Sheesh," Max added.

"Come on, I packed you both fruit and yogurt for the car. If you want a sit-down breakfast, you have to wake up earlier."

"Mom, you're supposed to wake us up," Max said.

"Remember how I taught you about those things called alarm clocks? You're old enough to take responsibility for your morning routines. You know that!"

We piled into our used Volvo, the Los Angeles sunshine breaking through the palm trees. Though I'd lived in LA practically my entire life, I still couldn't get over how insanely beautiful it was. The two years I'd spent in Seattle postcollege as an author's assistant was like living in a Weather Channel warning zone. I couldn't wait to get back to LA.

I barely managed to get in the car without spilling my travel coffee mug, which was *just* big enough *not* to fit in the cupholder *(Who makes this stuff?!)*, or dropping the on-the-go breakfast, my unzipped wallet, or the key fob, which didn't even plug in anywhere. Zoe was in the front seat next to me, the ice in her massive Hydro Flask water bottle clinking as she shoved it in between the armrest and center console, perilously close to my coffee. Max buckled up in the back and started taking selfies.

"Seriously, Max. Are you sending that photo of you somewhere? You didn't even brush your hair."

"I'm Snapping with my friends. That's what we do."

I sighed.

"Honey, why do your friends need to see you or the car window?"

"It's not *what* we Snap. It's just how often we do it."

He continued. "Mom, how come you never cook us breakfast? You always seem so busy."

Ouch.

Zoe ignored him. "Hey, what do you think about my getting a tattoo of H$_2$O on my arm? I'm so into water bottles. Then I'd never forget."

"There are so many reasons why that's a bad idea. I don't even know where to start. How about the fact that you can't get buried in a Jewish cemetery if you have a tattoo?"

She shrugged. "Cremation, baby."

I just sighed.

Max leaned forward from the backseat, not even responding to what I'd said. "Can I play a song? I need to hook up the AirPlay."

I leaned out of the way as Max's body smushed me all the way to the window.

"I mean, can you just—"

"Max, *I* was about to play a song," Zoe protested.

Max raised his voice a notch. "It's my turn, I was about to—"

"GUYS. STOP."

I slammed on the brakes at the stop sign and took a deep breath.

"Do you want me to get into an accident?! Sit down. Keep your seat belts buckled. And let. Me. Drive. Okay?"

I swear I used to be nice. Calm, happy, cheerful. My smile even lit up the room. A small room. But work and kids were wearing me down. I knew I would regret this outburst in about three minutes and then feel guilty throughout their entire school day. But I just couldn't control myself. My frustration. At everything.

From the backseat, Max whispered, "You can't say 'guys.'"

———

I grabbed the steering wheel in a death-clutch, my knuckles almost popping out of my skin—which, by the way, suddenly looked a little looser and more wrinkled than I remembered. *Not the time. Will deal with that later.*

Aging was coming on fast in my forties, as if someone had said, "Go!" and hurled bottles of stem-cell cream my way. The wrinkles?

Botox wasn't my thing. I know, I was the only one in LA who didn't use lasers or peels or chemicals or wraps or whatever, but after my mom's first attempt at Botox, when she got a near-fatal infection (bad) and had to endure bruising and discoloration all over her face for a month (worse), I decided it was better to be safe than sorry. I didn't want my obit—not that I would even get one—to be "Aging one-hit-wonder author dies in freak Botox incident." Too pathetic to contemplate. Wrinkles were a better alternative. My eyesight was also declining. One minute I could see fine, 20/20. The next? I couldn't tell which was the shampoo and which was the conditioner. Fine print? Forget it. Eyebrow tweezing? A joke.

I turned to the backseat.

"Max," I began. "First of all, I cook you guys—sorry, you *two*—breakfast all the time. Remember the eggs I made *yesterday*? Second of all, why don't you ever ask your dad to cook breakfast? He doesn't have to sleep in every day. Third, you're old enough to cook your own breakfast. And fourth, yes, I'm busy because I'm working!"

"Dad sleeps late because he works late, Mom," Max said. "He's at the theater rehearsing after I go to bed."

Ethan's child-actor days had peaked with the middle-grade sitcom *Crazygate* about a group of misfits who took over their school. He had been Misfit #2. And yes, his BMW license plate read "MZFIT2." Those Misfits were supporting our entire lifestyle. His theater job? Not so much.

"I mean, I work late, too."

"But from home, Mom. That's totally different."

"Is it?"

Ethan was a night owl anyway. So what if he had to go see a bunch of plays and help with rehearsals? How quickly Max always jumped in to defend him.

But maybe Max was right. Recently all I'd done was stare at my laptop. *Was* I really still an author if I wasn't writing? Could that mantle be stripped from my shoulders like a hair-salon cloak being whisked away?

Every good book idea I came up with had already been taken. How many original plotlines could there even *be*? Around a hundred thousand new novels came out each year. Was there even enough material to go around?

"I'm still having a tough time after the whole *Podlusters* fiasco."

"Mom, come on," Zoe said, fixing her hair in the visor mirror. "That was, like, *forever* ago. I didn't even *know* Todd back then."

"Wait, Todd from last night with the other girl?"

"Mom!"

My most major writing setback had come last March, and I still had plot-twist PTSD. I'd been on a roll since my New Year's resolution to write a thousand words a day, no matter what. Other authors always said that's how they got their books written. That and "Just put your butt in the chair and write."

I'd had a great idea for a novel over the previous school holiday break. I'd been chatting on the phone with Gabriela while lounging by the pool at Sunshades, the all-inclusive Hawaiian resort that Ethan's brother, Brad, ran; he always got us in for free. The kids and Ethan were surfing, so I had all the time in the world to chitchat.

"Hey, so how many of these 'podcasts' have you been on?" Gabriela asked.

"Podcasts? Oh, I don't know. Maybe fifty? Seventy-five? Why?"

"Ah. I need you to introduce me to a podcaster. I found him on Instagram. He is . . . Well, even his bookshelves are gorgeous. Mwah! Those abs. I can't. And I don't even read these days." Gabriela's flirtations had really escalated lately; her husband's lack of attention and constant travel certainly didn't help.

I laughed.

"Gabriela, you speak, like, five languages and were a comp lit major. If nothing else, you're in our book club!"

"I have four kids! Reading—bah! Hold on."

Her voice grew muffled as she yelled at her sons: "Stop jumping on each other! I don't care if you say it's the rules!" She resumed. "Sorry.

These boys with their sticks. These hard yellow balls are going to kill someone. Ridiculous."

"Lacrosse?"

"Yep."

"Not everyone can be as gifted a swimmer as you, my dear," I said.

"Yeah, yeah," she said.

"So what podcaster were you asking about?"

"The one with the gorgeous bookshelves. I think his show is called *Under the Hardcovers*."

"That's funny."

"The word 'hard' in there . . . Perhaps it's not an accident!" she said with a mischievous laugh.

"Hold on. Let me look." I opened Instagram to @underthehard-covers. "Wow."

A slew of close-ups of whoever this hardcover hunk was streamed down my screen. The greenest eyes, tan skin, perfect stubble, six-pack, and hair-free chest, plus rippling forearms holding fabulous books.

"Where did you *find* this guy?" I asked.

"My au pair told me about him. She says back home he's 'the biggest deal ever.'"

After thirty-plus years, "home" was still Venezuela.

"Sorry, Gabriela, I don't know Mr. Hardcover."

"Shoot. I have to get on his show!"

"Get on his show? Why?"

"How else will I meet him?"

I chuckled. "Gabriela, maybe you should write a book *just* to get on his show! He only interviews authors, right?"

"YES! My brilliant friend. Great idea. But . . . you and Kelly are the real writers. I gave up journalism after college. Now I write . . . what? Love letters. Permission slips. Playdate notes . . ."

I sat up on the chaise lounge.

"Wait. Gabriela! I love this idea: a woman with a crush on a pod-caster decides to write a book just to get on his show! A perfect meet-cute. I need to write this story."

"Yes! I love it. But then, can you say *I* wrote it?"

"No, no. I'm under contract for a new book. You know that. I need this! I can dedicate it to you, though?"

"*Really?* Thank you! But . . . then you haven't really solved my problem. And books take, like, fifty-seven years to come out. Okay, how about you just tell him about the book, and we go on his show together for research."

I was already standing up, throwing on my old Tina Turner T-shirt and frayed jean shorts over my bathing suit and grabbing my straw bag.

"I love you, Gaby."

Totally inspired, I'd flip-flopped right back to the hotel suite, typing ideas on my phone as I shuffled. Later, while Zoe was watching TikToks (how many skin-care videos could one teenager watch and still not have clear skin?!) and Max was playing tennis with Ethan, I quickly outlined the whole thing and started writing. I was *in it*. I'd finally nailed my plot for the *Poppies* follow-up. *Podlusters*. Maybe all my books could start with the letter *P*. It would be my thing! Pippa and the *P* books! Or maybe I was losing my mind.

That night at dinner, at a table in the sand lit by bamboo torches, the Hawaiian breeze gently swaying the tablecloths, I told the kids and Ethan my idea.

"Couldn't the main character just call up the Instagram guy and ask to be on his show?" Ethan said. "Why write a whole book?"

"No, these book podcasters are pretty strict. You can't just call and make an appointment like it's the orthodontist. Anyway, I think it'll be so much fun to write." I smiled at the kids. "What do you two think?"

They'd all gotten a little color, but I still looked like death thanks to my day unexpectedly writing indoors. We looked uniformly cheerful, though. The bright-orange leis around our necks made it official: we were on vacation.

"Make sure to get the Instagram handle," Zoe said. "It's probably already taken."

"Ohhhh, good point," I said, reaching for my phone.

"I thought 'no phones at the table,' Mom?" Max said.

I smiled and put it down.

"You're right! See? I was just testing you. You passed! Way to go, Max."

I reached over and ruffled the top of his hair, then stroked the back of his hand and gave it a squeeze. He rolled his eyes—but smiled. What a cutie. My little guy. The collar of his navy polo was uneven, his hair messy, and his skin a bit too pink from the sun, but what a *love*.

"I think it's a cool idea, Mom," Zoe added. "Now you just need to *write* it."

"I know, I know. I know!"

"Seriously, Pippa," Ethan added, rolling up the sleeves of his button-down shirt. "You've gotta be a good role model for the kids here. Show them you don't give up."

"What about you? Can't *you* try to be a good role model, too? It would certainly inspire the kids to see one of their dad's plays take the stage as well . . ."

"Mom, cut it out," Zoe said, putting her arm around Ethan's shoulders. "Dad is creative. He's always working!"

"Mm-hmm. That's what he tells himself at all the industry parties around town."

"Guys!" Max said. "Stop."

Zoe blurted, "You can't say—"

"I know!"

I put my face in my hands. "Just, everyone. Stop!"

# Four

M y mother always said, "Darling, it's not a *vacation* with kids; it's a *trip*." When I got home, my fingers continued to fly on the keys. "This podcast book is going to be a hit," I thought. I could feel it. I sat alone in my office, the house quiet with the kids in school and Ethan either sleeping, working out, or working. I couldn't help but chuckle at the ridiculous scenarios I put my characters into as the word count went up and up and up every day. I was in the zone! Finally! I could turn in my next novel by the summer for sure. I barely had time for open-house snooping, but I managed to sneak out a few times to showings in Cold Water Canyon and Malibu.

One June morning, after working diligently for months and producing 183 solid pages *(Yes!)*, I'd gotten up to grab a coffee during that 10:30 a.m. lull—and my career basically ended.

As the Keurig squeakily released the brew into my mug from that new bookshop in Santa Monica, I overheard Kevin from *Good Morning, Coffee Lovers, with Kevin and Cindy!* interviewing Southern sensation Ella Rankin, the #1 *New York Times* bestseller seventeen times over. I poured a splash of oat milk in my coffee and tuned in.

"Kevin," said Ella in her deep accent. "I'm just deeee-lighted to reveal my cover here today on *Good Morning, Coffee Lovers*. I've really kept this project under wraps!!"

"And we're excited to hear about it!" Kevin said, flashing his perfect white teeth.

"Not only will this book come out just in time for summer," Ella continued, "but it has already been optioned by Daydream Productions and is slated for film release next year!"

"Ella, we are *thrilled*! Aren't we, Kevin?" his angelic-looking cohost, Cindy Sweetheart, chimed in.

I rested my elbows on the kitchen island, cupping my mug, anticipating her big news.

"Cindy, yes! Very excited," Kevin added. "We're ready. Are you ready at home?"

Kevin looked right at me.

"Sure, Kevin," I said.

Kevin and Cindy started counting down on screen like it was New Year's Eve.

"Ten . . . nine . . . eight . . . seven . . . six . . . five . . . four . . . three . . . two . . . one . . . COVER REVEAL!"

No.

No. No. No.

I gasped. There, on national news, was the cover for Ella's new book.

With my title.

*Podlusters.*

The cover featured a dreamy dude in front of color-categorized bookshelves and a blonde woman at a laptop looking toward him, with heart emojis surrounding them.

"Are you kidding me?" I screeched.

"Ella, tell us about your book," Cindy said, smiling brightly.

"Oh, I'd love to, Cindy," Ella started. "Well, as you know, in addition to being a bestselling author, I'm also a podcaster. You know, so I can help the writing community. We all need a leg up, don't we?"

She smiled and Cindy smiled back, nodding.

"Bitch," I said.

"But to be on *my* podcast, *Subtext*, you have to write a book so we can talk about it! Well, this one man just would *not* leave me alone. He kept texting and DMing and calling, asking to be on my show . . . and instead of getting a restraining order"—she paused and laughed, tossing her high blonde ponytail behind her shoulders—"I told him, 'Well, honey, you're just gonna need to write a book, aren't you?'"

I screamed: "ARE YOU KIDDING ME?!"

Kevin and Cindy fake-laughed at this story about her stalker.

My phone started ringing. Kelly.

"ARE YOU KIDDING ME?"

"Shh, let's watch," she said.

"And then what happened, Ella?" Cindy asked, leaning in.

"Well, then, I thought, 'What a funny idea for a book! I think I'll write that next.' And here it is!"

"And just like that," Kevin said, motioning to the cover.

"And just like that!" Ella repeated. "I just whipped this book out in a few weeks, and here it is!"

The camera panned back to show an entire bookcase filled with copies of *Podlusters*.

"Thief!" I cried. "She stole my idea!"

"You know, she probably just had the *same* idea," Kelly countered.

"No way! It's too specific."

Ella continued. "Yep, it comes out on Memorial Day!" She turned to the camera. "And I hope all of you, especially my beloved fans at home, will preorder *Podlusters* right now!"

I shook my head. I could already hear the sales churning, her new book hustling up the bestseller charts like a salmon swimming upstream.

"Ella, what about the man?" Cindy asked. "The one who wanted to be on your show?"

"Oh, well, sadly he's gone to prison, but at least we all got a book out of it, didn't we?"

Cindy and Kevin laughed nervously.

"This is so messed up," I said.

Kevin looked into the camera. "Next up: Which actors use body doubles for sex scenes? Find out, after the break."

I dropped my head into my arms and moaned.

"Nooooooo!"

*All that work! My next big hit. Gone. Taken!*

"You'll think of something else," Kelly said. "You always do."

"No . . . I won't . . . I'm doomed!"

Texts started dinging in rapid-fire, like a Vegas slot machine. I ignored all of them. LeeLee's urgent texts. Sidonie's note, Well, looks like we're starting over.

*She* wasn't starting over. *I* was starting over. But how? Had someone betrayed me, or was it just a coincidence? Seriously, how could Ella Rankin have had the exact same idea? And shouldn't there be a cap on how many novels one author was allowed to write anyway?! Now my fun *P* book, inspired by *my* friend Gabriela, was taken! And Gabriela hadn't even met @underthehardcovers!

I called Gabriela.

"I'm about to start a session with my trainer. Can I call you after?"

I flashed back to college Gabriela, racing to the pool at school.

"I thought your hottie trainer went back to Sweden."

"This one is new," she said, giggling. I could hear a man laugh, too.

"Oh boy. Specific details later, please. But, Gaby, remember when you called me about @underthehardcovers and I decided to write *Podlusters*?"

"Of course! My claim to fame in the Pippa Jones career journals."

"Did you tell anyone else about the idea first? Or just me?"

"I can't really remember. Probably just you. Maybe Kelly? Josie? I don't know. Oh! I have to go now. We're about to do child's pose."

"Isn't that supposed to come at the end of a workout?"

"Oh, we'll get a workout." And she laughed again while I shook my head. Gabriela's midlife transformation was so drastic, sometimes it felt like she was an entirely different person. Sex jokes from the restrained, focused athlete-scholar turned dedicated wife and mom? I was still getting used to it.

If it wasn't Gabriela, who else could have spilled the beans? My publicist? My agent? Someone at the publishing company? Kelly and Josie were like sisters. Who else had I even told?

I called my publicist. We needed a plan.

"Brittany, it's me, Pippa." Her long pause made me nervous. *Come on.* "Pippa Jones. Your author from Driftwood? *Poppies?*"

"Oh, PIP-pa! Hi!"

"Who told Ella Rankin about *Podlusters?* Did you?"

"Slow down. I don't like these accusations. I saw that on TV, too. *No one* told Ella Rankin about your book. It just seems like a very unfortunate coincidence. But from the publicity seat, it's her book. First on the news gets the prize. So you better get going on whatever else you're working on or it'll look like *you're* the one copying *her.*"

"Oh, come on. I'm a much better writer."

"I won't argue with you there, but seventeen of her bestsellers beg to differ."

"Some publicity support would be nice!"

"Just tellin' it like it is. Sales don't lie."

Informal digging on the potential culprit got me nowhere. After a few hours of rage and indignation, I perched in front of my laptop and dragged my whole draft into the trash, then I pressed Empty Trash. At least I got to hear the little crumpling paper sound as I cried.

And then I cried some more.

I'd been struggling to find a new topic ever since.

# Five

*Thirteen missed calls.*

I pulled out of the school parking lot, waving to a few parents I vaguely recognized but whose names I always forgot.

"Pippa! Hi!" a mom yelled out of her Porsche SUV.

"Oh, hi . . . you!" I was clearly missing a name in that sentence. I'd started calling everyone "honey" if they were under age twenty-one or "you" if they were older.

LeeLee, my agent, was obviously trying to get in touch with me. She only called with good or bad news. And this couldn't be good. Since the Ella Rankin debacle the previous June, I'd produced nothing. Except on Instagram. @openhousebandit was going gangbusters. I started driving down the pristine streets of the Pacific Palisades toward home and braced myself.

"Siri, call LeeLee."

Long pause.

Finally, "Okay. Calling Lisa."

What?!

"No, Siri. Cancel. Cancel! Stop!"

Siri was calling my mother-in-law.

I grabbed the phone and pressed Cancel, a beat too late. Lisa—Ethan's mom—was the *last* person I wanted to talk to, especially this morning. She checked in from her Long Island home constantly, her raspy voice betraying years of stolen cigarettes. She was overly involved with everything Ethan and his brother, Brad, did.

Aaaaand. Yep. Lisa was calling back. I pressed the big X on the Volvo's touchscreen. Good lord. It was like operating an IBM computer room. I knew I'd hear about *that* declined call for a while. She hated when I didn't pick up. I could imagine her message already.

"Pippa? Dar-ling! I see you called. I'm so happy! What a blessing! Call me back, dear. I'll be sitting right here. Waiting. Call me! Mwah! Still waiting!"

I tried my editor again.

"Siri, call LEEEE-LEEEE."

Pause.

"Okay. Calling LeeLee."

"Thank you!!" I said, as if praising a small child.

The phone rang as I drove toward our Cape Cod–style home. It looked like someone had surveyed the Hamptons with a drone, picked out the best-looking house, plucked it up with a carnival claw, and dropped it on our tiny plot of land. Too East Coast? Who cared? I'd stalked this home for years, and as soon as I saw it come on the market, I made an offer. Occupational perk of an open-house creeper, and those were my amateur days. Luckily, Ethan also loved it. I made sure never to post about it; this one was for me.

"Hello?"

Obviously, it was me. My name was surely flashing on her phone.

"Hi, LeeLee. It's Pippa. Calling you back?"

"Hey! Awesome. How are things?"

"They're good. How—"

"Okay, listen. We have an issue here."

"Don't beat around the bush. Who needs small talk anyway? I'm listening."

"Driftwood needs your book. Any book."

"I'm working on it. It's almost there," I lied.

34

"Pippa. We all know you came close with *Podlusters*. By the way, you must feel validated now that Ella's version sold over a million copies! You were on the right track! What an idea!"

I sighed. "Thank you?"

"But look. If you don't get your polished manuscript in by next Friday, Driftwood is going to cancel your contract."

I must have misheard. I was in the middle of Sunset, cars honking all around. An elderly gentleman in a Tesla drove by and gave me the finger. *Fabulous.* I gave a little chin nod. Why did everything in LA happen to me in the car? Well, because, LA.

"Next Friday? Wait, LeeLee, they can't just *cancel* my contract."

"I happen to have your contract right here. And in paragraph 13.1.a, it clearly states that if the author doesn't deliver the work by the specified time, the deal is subject to cancellation. And you are three years past the due date. Three *years*."

"I know, I know. I'm sorry. But I'm getting it to them! I can't be the only author who has missed their delivery date. Plus, they've already paid me the advance!"

"About that . . ."

"No, no, no," I said, wagging my finger in the air as I resumed driving. "That advance is long gone. We redid the pantry and turned it into my new office. And Ethan is still trying to get his play off the ground, so this is not the best time."

"The new office looks great on Zoom."

I smiled from the driver's seat. "Thank you."

"But they're going to ask for those funds back if you don't deliver a manuscript."

"WHAT?"

"Pippa, just do the work! Finish whatever you've got. It doesn't have to be perfect. But send it in."

I was pretty sure I'd said something similar to Zoe recently. But, come on, I didn't really *mean* it.

I took a deep breath.

"How close is it?" LeeLee asked.

"Close. Really close."

"Great! Phew. I was worried you didn't have anything at all."

I bit my lip.

"Friday?" she said.

"Okay. No problem. You'll have it then."

"Perfect. No excuses this time!"

"Of course not! Would I give you an excuse?"

Long pause.

"Fine, I won't this time."

"I hope it really knocks my socks off. Make it pop, Pippa. Make it stand out."

"Okay. Sure! Of course."

Click.

I pulled into my driveway.

"Hey Siri. Shoot me."

Pause.

"Searching for . . . shoot me. Found it. There are . . ."

# Six

I went straight for the cabinet and grabbed the glass jar of oversize chocolate chips. I was going to have to pull out the big guns for this one.

*Maybe I should start with an outline for the novel. And maybe I should use . . . paper!* There had to be some paper around here somewhere. I started opening and shutting cabinets, quickly closing many before the precariously balanced pots and pans could fall out. Somehow I could never remember where anything was in my own kitchen. Finally I found a few pieces of crumpled-up paper under some old Hebrew school homework of Zoe's. Her bat mitzvah had been three years earlier, which meant this stack of papers had been hiding there for at least that long. I really had to do some reorganization. But not today! Today was a writing day.

Zoe's bat mitzvah had been so much fun. We had all of our family and her twenty closest girlfriends for a luncheon at the Hotel Bel-Air. (Ethan's brother got us a discount.) It was genuinely meaningful—and the dessert buffet didn't hurt, especially the pastry swans floating in that decadent sea of fudge sauce. We weren't particularly religious—Reform, not Orthodox. For us, that meant showing up a few times a year for the High Holidays, lighting the Shabbat candles when we remembered, and hosting a Passover seder. Orthodox was something else entirely. But the Jewish values were the same: giving back, being kind, being "people of the book." And bar and bat mitzvahs were a nonnegotiable in our family.

In fact, I was totally overdue in getting Max to Hebrew school. I'd reserved his date with the temple ages ago (by third grade, and all the prime spots had already been taken) and had claimed the party space above the sanctuary, but Max wasn't exactly Torah-ready. And boy, was that date fast approaching. I'd let his after-school chess club get in the way of studying for too long. Oh well.

In the meantime, I looked forward to celebrating Shabbat with Ethan and the kids on Friday nights all week long. No matter what we were up to, how much fighting took place between us, or how busy we were, we always stopped to light the candles on the kitchen island, recite the three prayers, take sips of wine or seltzer, and rip hunks of challah, shoving them into our mouths before sitting down to dinner or going our separate ways. Whoever invented the Jewish rituals (God?) was one smart cookie. Wine and bread? Twist my arm.

But now, the candles long extinguished, I really had to get going on this outline. Did I have a *pen*? I performed an elaborate writing-implement-selection ceremony like a surgeon selecting her scalpel. I tested out a few. Debated ballpoint versus felt-tip. Couldn't decide between black and blue. Or maybe green?

"Pippa! Stop it," I said out loud. "Just sit down and write an outline."

I was starting to annoy myself.

Finally I took my advice and sat down at my desk. In clear letters, I wrote *OUTLINE*. And then underlined it. Twice. And waited for inspiration to strike.

Nothing.

Time to phone a friend. I tossed down the (green ballpoint) pen and grabbed my phone.

"I have a slight issue," I said when Josie picked up.

"Don't we all? Hold on, love. I'm just leaving the station. Bye, Hank. Billy."

I could hear the loud click-clack of Josie's heels tapping the marble lobby as she left the KRXV building, chatting with the security guards.

Josie took her time with literally everyone, charming them with her broad smile and warm, kind eyes. Nothing flustered her. She was calm, cool, and collected on and off the air.

Her car beeped. Again. And again.

"What, are you hacking into the White House or something? What's with all the beeps?"

"It's my new hybrid. I told you! Hold on. Climbing in."

"How was work?"

"Oh, you know. I had the early, early shift this morning, but at least I'm off work by nine a.m.! I interviewed the new young mayor. Boy, is *he* a doll. Then a B-list actress. Well, maybe C-list. Some podcaster came on with book recommendations. And then I did my usual cooking segment before we profiled a new minister at that famous downtown church."

"Sounds like it was a *good day, Boston*!"

"Funny."

"You're such a pro," I said, dumping my purse on the kitchen counter.

"Thanks, Pips. Okay, now I'm driving home. Can't *believe* that I've already worked six straight hours. My life! So, hit me. What's the issue?"

I grabbed a blue coffee mug from the shelf.

"Um, you know that book I've been writing since Ella Rankin stole my idea for the last one?"

"She didn't steal your idea. You had the *same* idea. But yeah. Where are you with it?"

"Well, okay. I'm going to be totally honest here. I have nothing."

"Nothing? Come on."

"I mean. I've written a few things but they're terrible. I've deleted it all."

"You have? Maybe it was good! Better than you think?"

I put a coffee pod in the Keurig and pressed Start.

"It wasn't. Well, I didn't totally delete the files, but I put them in my folder with all the other reject drafts. It's like the Island of Misfit Toys from *Rudolph the Red-Nosed Reindeer*."

"What's the Island of Misfit Toys?"

"From the Christmas special! The one with—"

"Okay, stop. I didn't watch that movie. And I don't know what toys you're talking about. But what I hear you saying is that you don't have a book."

"Right."

"And?"

"And my agent called and said if I don't have a draft in by next Friday, they're canceling my contract AND asking for my advance back."

"Can they do that?"

"Apparently, yes."

She whistled.

"Didn't you spend that on your new office?"

"Yes. Yes, I did."

"See, this is why I could never write a book. I like TV. TV is immediate. I'm on. It's on. Then it's over."

"Profound thoughts. Really helpful, thanks. And by the way, *you* should write a book," I said, grabbing the oat milk.

"Your career is falling apart and you want me to take on the same issue?"

"I mean, I think you have a great story to tell. But okay, sorry, sorry. Josie! What do I do?"

"Well, you either sit in that brand-new office of yours and type your little heart out from now until Friday, or you pull out some of those lost toys and package them up real nice or . . . you start looking for a new job."

I sighed and took a sip.

"Don't we have book club tonight?" Josie asked.

"Yes. Clearly, I don't have time for book club."

"We *always* make time for book club. See you at eight online. What're we drinking tonight?" We always paired the book with a relevant beverage. We mostly came for the booze and conversation.

"Well, the book is *Writers & Lovers* by Lily King," I said. "I think there's a lot of wine in that book."

"You *think*? Didn't you read it?"

"A while ago."

"Okay. Chardonnay?"

"Cabernet."

"Counting down. Now go write something. You wrote a bestseller, Pippa. This one should be easy!"

"I know. So why isn't it?"

I grabbed *Writers & Lovers* off the bookshelf and propped it next to my computer, my green pen and scratch paper beside it.

Come on. I could *do* this.

But . . . what if I could only do it once?

# Seven

What was *wrong* with me? Why couldn't I think of anything to write? I had endless ideas before *Poppies*. But success had cast a dry spell that had gone on for years. *Years!* Ella Rankin didn't sit around watching the cursor blink or worry about having her advance ripped away, right?

The workday was worthless. I kept brainstorming ideas and dismissing them immediately. I toyed with the idea of a woman who only posted the most unflattering photos of herself on Instagram, so whenever anyone met her, they were like, "Wow, you look amazing!" and her body perception morphed through the experiment. Then I tinkered with a novel set in the world of competitive backgammon, called *Lover's Leap*. How about a multigenerational saga about three women in a Jewish family who visit a vacation resort together? Some of my ideas had potential, but when I went to flesh them out and actually start, I froze. Where to begin?

The screen was still blank, and I only had a few hours before I had to pick up Max. The house was quiet, the dishwasher humming, the laundry spinning—just like my brain.

I scooched back my wheely chair and hit the wall. My new office was really just a small closet. It must have originally been designed for the type of woman who had multiple sets of china to arrange in an artful way, a woman who could walk in, take a few steps, twirl around, and still be surrounded by beautiful dishes. How did those women decide which china to use when? They didn't have more meals than the rest of us.

Instead of filling the space with beautiful dishes, I'd installed discount bookshelves all along the perimeter and filled them with books sorted by color. Well, I'd started to, until I gave up halfway through and just jammed the rest into the shelves. Photos of my kids filled the bulletin board in front of my desk, a gray-and-tan chevron wallpaper behind it. It was my happy place. I could do this.

I leaned forward.

*What if?* I typed.

*What if . . . the one you loved wasn't who you thought they were?*

Done. Too often.

*What if . . . the guy at the next restaurant table was your son but you didn't know it?*

Highly improbable. Maybe.

*What if . . . the bird tapping on my window right now is actually my dead grandmother and suddenly it transforms into her and—*

Stop. No.

"Forget it," I thought. "Time for an email break."

I closed out of the Word doc and scanned through the 327 emails, including some new listings and many kid-related missives. How did everyone else stay on top of their inboxes? Some days it just felt impossible.

*What if . . . there was a world without email . . .*

From the school: "Turns out we've picked the wrong day for professional day! We're switching from the 10th to the 9th." Great, there went my annual ob-gyn checkup.

"Storewide sale. Take 20% off!" *Oh yes! This.*

From Ethan, emailing me from bed upstairs: "Can we host three of the actors I might work with for dinner tonight? Otherwise, I'm going to head out to dinner with them." *Ugh.* Meanwhile, I'd had an entire day already—an unproductive one, but still—and he was still lounging?!

From Zoe's guidance counselor: "Don't forget to research summer program options to bolster Zoe's college applications. It matters!" Please. She was a *sophomore*.

From my mom: "Hi darling! Just checking in. Can you join us for Passover this year? It'll be at Caitlin and Will's in Scottsdale. Do join! Caitlin puts on *such* a lovely seder."

Wait, seriously? My cousin William and his (Catholic) wife, Caitlin, were hosting Passover? I lived two hours, max, away from my mom in the desert. Now we were supposed to schlep to Arizona? For what? To hang out with the shiksas of Scottsdale?!

"Pippa?"

Ethan was standing at the door, gray-ish hair disheveled, still in those horrible old pajamas.

"Yeah?"

"Did you get my email? Can we have dinner with those actors?"

"Sorry, I was just going through all my messages. Zoe has dance with Greta, and Max has chess, plus I have my book club with the girls. I can't do it. But maybe you can go?"

"Okay, I'll go. Thanks."

I felt a pinprick of jealousy.

"Anyone . . . special . . . in the group of actors? A leading lady?"

"Cut it out, Pippa."

Occasionally, I caught glimpses of the Ethan I first met. We'd both been eating at Locanda Veneta. He was with his mom, Lisa, and I was with Kelly back when we were living together in LA; she was doing all the West Coast tournament coverage.

"Isn't that the guy from that show?" Kelly asked, looking over in his direction. "Wow, he's so cute as a grown-up!"

"Oh yeaaaahh," I said, nodding. "That kid. The middle-school show!"

"He looks good," Kelly said, swirling her vodka soda with a plastic straw (when that was still a thing).

"Really good," I said, sipping my cosmopolitan as we glanced over the menus.

Our stares didn't go unnoticed. When Lisa got up to use the bathroom, she walked by our table and said in her smoker's voice, "If you gaze at my Ethan any more obviously, your eyes will fall out of your heads!"

We all laughed. Ethan got up and walked over to us.

"Oh no, what'd she say to you? I'm so sorry."

"No problem," I said.

"She totally called us out," Kelly added. "But we were just admiring the decor, right, Pippa?"

"Obviously," I said, smiling at him. He smiled back.

"Ethan," he said, extending his hand. "Nice to meet you."

"Pippa," I said. "Nice to meet you, too."

We locked eyes like in the movies, and he held on to my hand a beat too long.

I could hear Kelly clearing her throat, wanting her turn to say hello, but he was only looking at me.

"And this is Kelly," I added.

"Hi!"

"Hi," he said, barely looking at her.

"Looks like you all met. The staring worked. Ha!" Lisa said, walking back from the bathroom. "Ethan, come on. Let's get back to our spaghetti."

"One sec, Ma," he said. "Can I get your number?" Ethan said to me.

"Yes, of course," I said, blushing.

This was pre-cellphone days, so Ethan ran to the maitre d' station to grab a pen and a business card to write on.

While he was gone, Kelly quipped, "Playing hard to get, huh?"

"Shut up," I said, grinning.

I wrote my name and number on the card and handed it back to him. He glanced at it and said, "Perfect, Pippa. Let's hang out. I'll call you."

When he walked away, I covered both cheeks with my hands and pretend-screamed.

"You lucky duck," Kelly said.

Ethan called the next day, and we made plans to meet at the Chateau Marmont bar. I was so nervous, my legs were shaking. Was I dressed right? Would he be into me?

He waltzed in like he owned the place, greeting everyone who worked there like an old friend.

"Wow, so you're a regular?" I said, smiling.

"Something like that," he said. "I'm so glad you're here. I haven't stopped thinking about you."

I blushed.

"Come on."

"I mean it!"

I shook my head.

"Want proof?"

"Sure," I said.

He leaned over and kissed me, before we'd even ordered drinks. And it was . . . wonderful. We had incredible chemistry. I didn't want his lips to part from mine; they fit together perfectly. My heart was racing like mad, and I kind of forgot we were in the middle of a popular bar. It felt like the world had shrunk down to just him and me. The lack of foreplay? Soon that wouldn't be romantic, just annoying.

When he pulled away, grinning, I joked, "Well, that was forward of you."

"When you know, you know."

"How do I know you're not an axe murderer?"

"I didn't even get the part in *So I Married an Axe Murderer*. That's how far off you are."

He made me laugh. We had one drink in the dimly lit celebrity bar, then he asked if I'd like to see his room. Turns out, he was *living* there. At Chateau Marmont. Holding hands, we navigated the hallways until we got to his door.

When he opened it, I gasped. A bottle of champagne in an ice bucket. Sultry music playing. Rose petals scattered all over the bed.

"A little presumptuous?" I asked. "What if I'd said no to coming to your room?"

"Oh, I would've found someone else," he said.

"Hey!"

"But she wouldn't have been as special as you."

We didn't leave the room the entire weekend. It was steamy and hot and raw and messy and everything I'd ever longed for. He described what it was like to grow up famous and how it translated to some trust issues. He even got vulnerable, telling me about abuse he'd seen and experienced in the industry; his difficult relationship with his brother, Brad; and his lifelong dream of becoming a theater producer. Who knew!

As we lay in bed, the shades slightly ajar, letting in morning light, I rolled onto my stomach to look right at him.

"What was it like losing your dad so young?" I asked. "You don't have to talk about it if it's too upsetting."

He'd told me earlier that he was six years old when his father died suddenly of a heart attack in front of the whole family, but then he'd quickly changed the subject. I wanted to try again.

"Oh, it was awful. I couldn't sleep for months. I kept thinking that if I'd done something differently, like called 911 a few moments earlier, maybe he would have lived. God, I never talk about this," he said, his voice quivering.

"I'm so sorry," I said, stroking his cheek.

"And I felt so responsible. Brad was only four years old, and my mom . . . well, my mom was a mess. After the shiva, she barely got out of bed for months. I had to get Brad and me to the school bus and cook and all of it. Plus, we didn't have much money. That's why I decided to pursue acting. I couldn't think of any other ways to make money at that age. And I wanted to support my family."

"My gosh, the pressure you put on yourself," I said.

"I guess," Ethan said. "I worked with the drama teacher at school, and he helped me apply for different gigs. I started booking commercials, a few voice-overs, and then, the big one."

"Wow."

"My mom was so proud of me. I think it just really kept her going. I was so independent that she only really had to look after Brad."

"Where does Brad live now?" I asked.

"He's still living at home with Ma, taking care of her. But he wants to go into the hotel business. We'll see what happens."

"I'm glad he's there for her."

"I haven't thought about that time in a while," Ethan said. "It was really, really hard. I felt like I'd lost both my parents at once. I never really had a childhood after that, you know?"

I nodded.

And then his eyes filled with tears.

"It's okay. You can tell me anything," I said softly. "I'm here for you."

I nestled into his side with my arms around his middle as the West Hollywood sun rose high in the sky. He quickly pushed me away, but I thought it just meant he didn't want to be affectionate right then. It's funny how easy it is to miss warning signs. Like how he didn't even ask me about losing *my* dad. I was just a baby, but knowing that I lost him to pancreatic cancer was horrific.

For those first couple of months, we spent every night together at the Chateau. I started waving to the staff like a regular myself. Did I miss being at the apartment I shared with Kelly in Westwood? Not really, although I think she was annoyed at how little I was home.

Ethan proposed at the Chateau bar. He had Stan, the bartender, stop the music, and got everyone to clink their glasses and go quiet. And then, right at the bar, he got down on one knee.

"Pippa, will you spend the rest of your life with me?"

I couldn't stop smiling.

"I would be honored," I said, beaming.

It was just so *easy* between us. Of course, our moms didn't exactly get along; both of them were used to being the center of attention. But no bother. Everything else was moving along swimmingly. If only I'd known what was coming.

Now we'd been married seventeen years. *Seventeen. Long. Years.* I still respected him and was insanely attracted to him even though I wished I weren't. But his complete lack of physical affection and the brutal way he interpreted sex wore me down. Year after year. Until it felt like I was living a lie. One I kept close to the chest.

At first, Ethan seemed as crazy about me as I felt about him—and he showed it. But soon I would do something simple, like reach out to hold his hand as we walked down the street, and he'd recoil like I'd bitten him. Just a few months into our marriage, I had to confront him. I hated confrontation, but I just couldn't cry about it silently anymore. Why was he pulling away? Had I done something to upset him? Was I less attractive than when he met me? Had he lost interest? Was I bad in bed? Was it my body?

I remember the night so clearly. It was really late and I'd had a drink or two at dinner with Josie, who was working as a newbie on-air reporter in Orange County. I got into bed and tried to snuggle with him as he read a script beside me. I nuzzled into his neck, but he just patted my head without looking up, like I was a golden retriever, and moved away, and then ignored me. I rolled over, embarrassed. Ashamed. Why wouldn't he look at me? Touch me?

Our wedding gifts—useless kitchen gadgets I'd never learn to use (a "zester"?)—were still in boxes in our garage. It had been weeks and weeks of this particular type of rejection. I couldn't take it anymore.

I wiped my eyes, turned toward him, and whispered, "Ethan . . . is there someone else?"

"What?"

He didn't put down the script, just stared at it angrily.

"Have you fallen in love with someone else? Or is it something I did? You've totally stopped touching me . . ."

"What do you mean? We have sex all the time."

Blank

"I know, but I mean actually touching me. Holding me. Holding my hand even."

"Oh, come on. I'm just not like that."

"Like what? *Nice?* Loving?"

"I don't like to be touched. Or touch in general."

"Touch in general? As in one of the five senses? As a concept?"

I sat up straight, willing him to at least look in my direction while we spoke.

"Can you put down the script and discuss this? It's kind of a big deal."

"It isn't a big deal," he said, tossing the script on his bedside table. "Unless you make it one."

"It's just that you've flipped a switch. On our honeymoon and basically the entire time we were dating, you were affectionate . . . and it was amazing. But now . . ."

"I knew I had to do that stuff before."

"That *stuff?*"

"Like touching you, holding hands, and all that. Sex is different."

"Sex is different? What are you even talking about? Ethan, I didn't sign up for an entire life with no affection."

He looked over at me, nonplussed.

"Come on, Pippa. You know I love you. If I didn't, I wouldn't have married you. But no, I just don't like to be touched." He literally shivered. "It gives me the heebie-jeebies."

"The *what*?!"

"The heebie-jeebies. My mom always used that expression. It's when something gives you the chills or just disgusts you or something, like a haunted house." He laughed a little.

"So what you're saying is that the thought of your wife . . . me . . . touching you . . . makes you feel . . . like you're in a HAUNTED HOUSE . . . with your mom?"

"Well, no, I was just explaining what the heebie—"

"Don't say it again."

51

"Okay. Why are you getting so upset?"

I flung off the covers and got out of bed. Our bedroom, the one I'd lovingly painted the exact right shade of lavender, suddenly felt like a prison.

"Why am I getting upset? Listen, it's not like I need you to be all over me. But you've given me a death sentence over here. A husband who seemed like a loving, affectionate guy, who just months ago walked with me down the aisle in front of all our family and friends, at a wedding my mom put on—at considerable expense, I might add—is telling me it was an act?"

He sighed. "Not an act, per se. Just something I knew I needed to do. But now that it's done, I'd prefer not to. Okay? Jeez."

He picked up the script. "Are we done here, Pippa? What, you're going to divorce me because I don't want to hold your hand? How stupid would *that* be? Plus, I told you. I love you. You vowed to love me back in sickness and in health."

"A complete lack of physical affection isn't a sickness. It's just *mean*."

"I still want to have sex with you. But just not all that other touchy-feely stuff. In fact, now that we're talking about it, why don't you take off that T-shirt and climb up here."

He patted his lap and gave me a goofy grin.

"What? You just completely morphed into another person!" I said, pacing around the bed.

"Come on, you're hot! I'm attracted to you. So just stop talking about all this and get over here. Can't you see how excited I am?"

He gestured down to the blankets.

And that was the moment when a piece of me shriveled up and died. I'd married someone who *just* wanted to have sex with me. I thought back to all the times he'd slapped me during sex. I thought it had been done playfully. I thought it was hot, actually—an erotic move to keep things interesting. But that was *all* I was going to get. Quick and dirty. Now that I thought about it, he never looked at me when we did it. He didn't kiss me, and barely cuddled after.

Theoretically I could live without having actual intercourse for the rest of my life. But I couldn't live without touch: affection, cuddles, holding hands, sitting on his lap, nuzzling during movies, kisses, hugs. Could I? Without physical affection, all I'd feel was lonely. Touch was my love language.

Standing by the bed, I shook my head. "Now? Are you kidding?"

"Get over here," he said coyly. "Let me show you what I mean by love."

I wanted to cry. To process. To think through what he'd said. But looking at him, so deliciously sexy with his broad shoulders from years of weight lifting, his fit physique, I couldn't resist. Even when I was livid and heartbroken.

I slinked over.

"Fine. But show me you *actually* love me."

He smiled and I climbed under the covers.

"Get on top of me," he said. "Take off your shirt."

He was always bossy like that. I'd thought it was hot, but I'd missed the real message.

I threw my ratty T-shirt aside as he ground me on top of him, back and forth, back and forth, until he couldn't stand it anymore. Then he literally picked me up, flipped me onto my stomach, pulled me to the edge of the bed like a rag doll, yanked my pajama pants and underwear down, and forced himself into me. Pound, pound, pound. He slapped me as he went. Pound, pound, slap. Until he cried out, with one final push, and then pulled out quickly, panting.

"See?" he said as I lay there, my grip on the sheets slowly loosening. "I told you I love you," he said, chuckling.

He walked over to the dresser and put on a pair of pajamas as I peeled myself off the bed, shaking. He seemed so proud of himself. He spanked my ass one more time as I walked to the bathroom, then climbed into bed, turned off his bedside lamp, and went to sleep.

I slid open our bathroom door and sat on the toilet and held my breath, knowing how much it would hurt to pee—for days. This wasn't a sexy, sometimes hot, erotic routine of his. This was it. This was all it was ever going to be. No kisses. No cuddles. Transactional sex. Nothing for me. For him, this was love.

———

Over the next couple of years with Ethan, I did everything to make him see my point of view, but I was so ashamed by his rejection that I didn't tell a soul. He agreed to marriage counseling, but it didn't help. I went to a sex therapist, who just looked at me with sympathy and said, "This is not predictive of a successful marriage." No advice. No tips for moving forward.

But what? I was going to leave my charming, sexy husband because he didn't want to hold hands and cuddle? Who did that? Marriage was about a lot of things. For me, it just wouldn't involve love, at least not the kind of love I envisioned. I certainly wasn't the only wife in *that* predicament. I tried to accept it. I shoved my needs deeper and deeper until I didn't even know what they were anymore.

When it came time to try for kids, I found out that I had a rare condition: my reproductive age was forty-five, although my body was only thirty. I wouldn't be able to have children on my own. Having our two children via IVF put yet another wedge between us, even though we were both dying to have kids—that was one thing we were always in agreement about. But now there was *literally* no need for him to touch me. He just had to show up at the doctor's office, deposit his specimen, and leave. He didn't even come to any of my other appointments, saying the process "creeps me out."

We went through many failed rounds, and I mourned the loss of those little cell clusters deeply. But Ethan just looked at it pragmatically. He'd shrug and say it was just about the odds. Why was I so upset? We'd try again.

Sex ceased almost completely. Every so often, when I was at my most depressed, he'd toss out a throwaway line: "You know I love you."

Did I? Did he? He wouldn't even hug me when I cried. It was like being married to a stranger.

We went about our lives together as colleagues with benefits. Our relationship was pretty conflict-free on the outside, even in front of our kids. But I knew our secret. My physical and emotional needs were never addressed. Apparently they just weren't on the table. No warm, kind, loving touch would ever pass between us.

Why didn't I leave? Why didn't I tell my girlfriends? I was too ashamed by how deeply unattractive I must be. How dumb I'd been not to notice any of this before it was too late. I'd vowed to stay with him for life, so that's what I was going to do. But no one warned you that sometimes those vows can be toxic.

# Eight

You working on your book?"

Ethan stood in the office doorway just before I was planning to get up to pick up the kids from school.

"Yep, working on my book," I lied.

He knocked on the doorframe and turned to head out. "I'm headed to Erewhon for a turmeric latte. Want one?"

"No thanks," I said. "Actually . . . we might have a slight issue with my advance . . ."

"Tell me when I get back. Need coffee!" he called as he walked out the door.

I yelled back: "Isn't a turmeric latte, like, seventeen dollars? You know, there's a coffee machine in the kitchen!"

He walked back into my office.

"We're fine, Pippa. We can afford *coffee*. Did you forget that you're Pippa Jones, bestselling author?"

"I don't even think there's coffee in a turmeric latte. You're basically paying for herbs and spices."

He rolled his eyes and walked out.

"Wait, one more thing," I said. "Before your dinner, is there any way you could pick up Max so I can get Zoe and go to book club?"

"Sorry. I'm going to check out an actress in a new student production at USC beforehand. She's supposed to be the next big thing. It's on the calendar."

Ah, the dreaded calendar. That was also my fault. I'd started a color-coded Apple iCal for each kid, for him, for my various commitments, for the hourly blocks that ruled our lives. He then added in his own work calendar, which I was supposed to stay apprised of. But I usually forgot to check either of ours. Of course he couldn't pick up the kids. Couldn't, or wouldn't?

I turned back to my desk and faced the screen. He loved me. I was lucky. Right?

As I sat unproductive at my desk, summoning my subconscious to perform on command like a circus animal, I thought—with a dramatic sigh—about all the other ways my life could have gone. The boyfriends I didn't marry. The kids I didn't have. The paths I hadn't taken. What would my life be like and who would I be? Maybe I should write about that, some sort of *Sliding Doors* spin-off.

I thought back to when Zoe was ten and Max was seven and they didn't have school so I'd driven them to Universal. Maybe it was teacher training day or faculty appreciation day or another new holiday that suddenly popped up on the calendar. I think the administration liked to throw in random Wednesdays off just to mess with the parents' work schedules, as if to say, "See how *you* like it when kids mess up your entire day."

So I'd driven them to the Burbank area. A road trip! From the west side of LA! They even threw their sleeping bags in the trunk.

Zoe seemed unusually quiet. She'd just graduated to sitting shotgun, thanks to an early (and, as we later realized, only) growth spurt. Max was sitting in the back, shuffling through his Pokémon album.

I could tell that Zoe was trying to say something; she kept turning to me and starting to talk, then shifting back into her seat and looking out the window. After it happened a couple of times, I finally said, "Okay, love. Either you have to go to the bathroom, you've suddenly forgotten the English language, *or* there's something that you're afraid to say out loud."

She put both hands over her face and giggled. Then she leaned over and whispered, "How did you know?"

"Um, maybe because I've spent the past ten years watching you, feeding you, putting you to bed . . ."

"Okay, okay," she said.

"Spill it."

She took a deep breath.

"Mom, did you ever . . ."

She stopped again.

"What? It's okay, love. Just ask. I'm an open book. You know that!"

Another deep breath. "This better be good," I thought.

"Did you ever . . . have . . . a crush on anyone?"

I turned and looked at her beautiful face, her eyes searching me in such a vulnerable way, her forehead creased, the wisps from her ponytail framing her eyes.

"Oh my gosh, *yes*," I said, laughing. "I had so many crushes!" Then I whispered, "Do *you* have a crush on someone?"

"I think so."

She bit her lip. (I kept forgetting to make her that orthodontist appointment. Mental note: schedule!)

"It's okay to have a crush, love. It's totally normal!"

"Who was *your* first crush?" she asked.

"Yeah, who was it?" Max added. "Gross."

"You really want to know?" I asked. Sometimes I was surprised when the kids took an actual interest in me as a person and not just a mom.

"Yes!" they said.

"Okay, okay! Well, my first big crush was on a boy I went to sleep-away camp with. I went to the girls' camp and he went to the boys' camp, but every night there was something called 'fence' where the camps could hang out. I would always look for him and then, like, run away when he got too close."

59

"Did you ever talk to him?" Zoe asked. Both kids were leaning in, listening closely.

"Well, one of my friends told him I had a crush on him, which was completely mortifying. I kept avoiding him after that; I was so embarrassed that he knew! But then at the camp dance, he walked straight over when the first song came on—the song was 'Stairway to Heaven,' by the way—and asked me to dance! I was *dying*. Dying!"

Zoe laughed.

Max asked, "Did you say yes?"

"I said yes! And we started slow dancing . . ."

"What's that?" Max looked confused.

"Oh, slow dancing is when the two people dancing have their hands on each other's shoulders and waists and kind of sway to a slow song. Anyway, I noticed that he smelled funny—not bad, just . . . funny. I recognized the smell but couldn't place it. I thought maybe it was a new shampoo or something. Since I didn't know what to say, I asked, 'Are you wearing cologne?' And he said, 'No, why?' And I said something like, 'You smell nice.' And before I could get too embarrassed for saying that, he said . . ." I started laughing.

"He said *what*, Mom?" Zoe said.

"Mom, come on! Tell us!"

I giggled again. "Okay, okay. He said, 'I put deodorant on my face so I wouldn't sweat. That's probably what smells nice.'"

"He did *what*?"

I laughed again, remembering the whole scene.

"Can't you just picture us? I was in this cute little striped, short-sleeve dress and flats, a red headband, and blue eyeliner that my counselor let me borrow. He was—and I remember this like it was yesterday—he was wearing two polo shirts, one over the other, with both collars turned up."

"Why?"

"I have no idea!"

"With deodorant on his face?"

"Yes!" I started laughing so hard, I had to wipe my eyes. "And when he talked to me about, I don't know, archery, I can't remember, I realized that maybe I actually *didn't* have a crush on him. I had imagined him a certain way, but every time he opened his mouth, I was like, 'Oh no. Just stop.'"

"Mom!"

"I know! My crush was crushed!"

"So then what happened?"

"Then I ended up dancing with his friend, who was really nice. And the friend and I ended up not dating but spending a lot of time together and, well, flirting, I guess. He was super nice. But my original crush? Poof. Gone."

"What was his name?"

"My first crush? I think it was Fred. I can't totally remember."

"What about the friend?"

"The friend . . . gosh. I can't remember his name at all. Isn't that terrible? James? Jonah? It'll come to me."

"And that was your only crush?"

"No, no, I had so many. I'd get all nervous, my heart would pound, I wouldn't know what to say, all that. You, too?"

"Yep."

"So who's the lucky guy?"

"Wait, you have a crush on someone, Zoe?" Max asked.

"Shut up, Max."

"Hey!"

I intervened. "Don't say 'shut up,' Zoe. Come on, apologize to Max."

"Sorry, Max."

"Say it like you mean it this time. Just because you're feeling a little embarrassed about something doesn't mean you should take it out on him."

"Okay, fine. Max, I'm sorry. I shouldn't have said that."

"Shit!" I yelled.

"MOM!"

"Sorry, sorry! I missed the exit on the freeway! Oh God, we're heading toward downtown. *Shoot*."

While I figured out how to get back en route, Zoe sat smiling next to me.

"Oliver Fisher," she finally said.

"What about him?"

"That's my *crush*, Mom. Jeez."

"Oliver Fisher! No way. His mom used to have you over for playgroup."

"Really?"

"Yes! I think I have pictures of you and Ollie as babies somewhere. I'll show you."

She giggled. "Well, that's my crush. But Jenna says he might have a crush on Ava."

"How would Jenna know?"

"Jenna knows everything about everyone."

"Well, keep *her* around," I joked.

"Mom, did you have other boyfriends before Dad?" Zoe asked.

"I did!"

"Gross," Max quipped.

"A lot?" Zoe asked.

"Not a lot. A few."

"What were their names?" she continued.

"Oh, come on. You really want to know?"

"YES!" Max and Zoe both said emphatically.

I debated what to share. I'd wanted a boyfriend all through high school, especially as my other girlfriends paired off. By the end of senior year, I started to wonder if I'd ever have a real boyfriend. Maybe something was wrong with me? I was so deeply ashamed to graduate without being in a real relationship. I wouldn't tell the kids this, but I was so desperate to prove that I wasn't *totally* unattractive that I fell into things with a new college classmate, Chris, way too quickly. He was the first guy who really liked me. He was a first-generation Indian American, recruited to Bluestone University for the baseball team.

When I told my mother about him, she'd waited a beat and then said dramatically, "Well, I do love chicken curry."

Everything out of her mouth made me cringe. If only I could delete her inappropriate, unfiltered comments.

Chris was probably the root of my toxic relationships to follow. It was most likely my deep, lingering shame over not having a boyfriend for so long that made me settle for anyone, just to feel remotely attractive and accepted.

Even when Chris publicly kissed another girl in the middle of a fraternity party, I took him back after he apologized.

"It meant nothing! I was totally drunk! I don't even remember! Please! I love you. You're everything to me."

And when he did it again a few months later at the campus bar, I still gave him another chance. He'd always come crawling back, saying, "Please don't leave me. I have a problem. It's like a compulsion. I don't want to be with anyone but you. I love you. Please. Help me work through this."

And I would stick by his side. That's what good girlfriends did, right? I had to help. I was loyal! And, I loved him, at least as much as I understood love.

And then Chris went too far. Not only was he kissing other girls and then crying about how he was always sabotaging a good thing (crazy that *I* would console *him* after he cheated on me), but he was doing terribly in school. All the drinking, the partying, the sports, the lifelong pressure from his parents, it toppled him.

One afternoon he came into my dorm room looking like a ghost.

"What happened?" I asked.

"I was accused of cheating."

"What? What proof do they have?"

He just hugged me and started crying. He was always crying. I should've recognized it all as manipulation, but what did I have to compare it to?

"Chris?" I repeated my question. "What proof do they have?"

"You have to help me," he whispered.

"Of course, I'll help you. I love you! But you have to tell me what happened."

"Plagiarism. Of an English paper."

"What, exactly, did you plagiarize?"

He looked me in the eye. His were red from crying. "I can't tell you."

"Come on. You can tell me anything." I stroked his face, trying to seem calm, but I was outraged. *Cheating?*

"I, uh. Oh boy." He cleared his throat. "I took one of your papers. From last year. You're so good at writing! So I went into your computer and changed my name in the file and submitted your essay."

"Oh my god."

I released my grip and backed away. This could sink me, too.

"We can find a way out of this," he said. "We can say our papers just got switched in the printer or something!"

"You want me to cover for you?"

"Otherwise I'll be expelled. And my life will be ruined. All our long-term plans to be together, how will we do that?"

What choice did I have? I did love him, and I couldn't just switch that off. Plus, if he got expelled, then I could never break up with him. And what would I do? Stay in the relationship? Long distance?

Maybe it wasn't *such* a big deal, I rationalized. I'd never cheated in my life. Hard work was everything to me. But so were love and loyalty. I was in an impossible situation. If I covered for him, it would be unethical. If I didn't, I was essentially destroying the love of my life.

And so, I allowed him to say it had been an honest mistake. That the files were labeled incorrectly in the computer and he just printed mine by mistake. I went with him to the campus disciplinary hearing and stood in the wood-paneled campus room in front of a semicircle of professors and peers, and vouched for him. Somehow I convinced the board to drop the case.

Chris wasn't expelled but was quietly suspended. He was allowed to graduate with our class and didn't even have to tell prospective employers about it.

As it turns out, he broke up with me a few weeks before graduation, claiming he couldn't look me in the eye after what happened. He was moving to the East Coast to try his hand at finance. I was staying in California. It would never work.

But after four straight years of that emotional, draining mess, I couldn't seem to find my way back to a healthy relationship. Maybe Ethan's lack of affection was just par for the course.

Back on the freeway, I told the kids, "I dated a boy named Chris in college, but he and I went our separate ways after graduation."

"*Then* who did you date?"

"Then I dated a very nice man named Brendan. He was a med student training to be a doctor. But I barely saw him. He lived at the hospital. I spent most of our relationship going out with my girlfriends. So we broke up, too. But now he's a very successful orthopedic surgeon, which means he fixes peoples knees, shoulders, hips, all that."

"And then Daddy?"

"Actually, yes. And then Daddy."

We pulled into Universal and I parked the whole conversation. Maybe I could write a novel with Zoe called *Crushed* about a daughter's first crush and her mom's crushing disappointment in love?

I jotted down the idea. Zoe would hate it.

# Nine

"Who wants to start?"

Zoom book club was about to begin. The kids were doing homework upstairs, Ethan was out at his all-important dinner, and I was clutching a goblet of cabernet. I was sitting at my desk, clad in my oversize gray Malibu Farm hoodie, my hair in a high pony, my makeup long gone. It was still early evening in LA, the sunshine just dimming. The books behind me were illuminated like in a David Hockney painting.

"I'll go," said Kelly.

"Overachiever," I joked.

"Always number one?" Gabriela added.

"Whoa," Kelly said, smiling. "Fine. I'll go *last*. Way to punish a girl for being assertive. So off-brand, ladies."

"We're kidding, Kel," said Josie. "Go ahead."

"Well, I *loved* the book."

Kelly launched into her interpretation of Lily King's masterpiece from the edge of her living room on Fifth Avenue in Manhattan. Her understated classic six was filled with family antiques, framed photos of her kids at "the club," and assorted floral wallpapers. It was always perfectly clean, as if her three kids, after full days at the single-sex Spence and Buckley schools and then tournament training all evening, barely walked through the house, let alone lived there. Sisal carpets and faded fabrics gave off the impression of their not trying too hard, but the whole aesthetic was carefully orchestrated. The goal? Wealth so understated it was hardly evidenced. A few oil portraits of Kelly's mom and grandmother as little girls in pink dresses next to their horses were subtly scattered about, as were black-and-white portraits of her own kids. A beat-up handed-down baby grand piano showcased more silver-framed pictures of her smiling kids and photogenic husband at the beach.

Some days it was hard to be friends with Kelly. Everything always seemed perfect and easy for her family. If I didn't love her so much, I'd probably unfollow her. Kelly hadn't just won the genetic lottery; she then had to conquer the literary scene with her thriller series, too. And she was genuinely nice. And thin. "I just don't care about food," she'd explain. What?!

I mean, really. What *didn't* she have?

"I loved the novel, too," Josie said, "but what about the older male author character? Did he seem believable to you?"

Boxes stacked behind her, Josie was Zooming in from her latest furnished rental in Boston—yet another temporary spot she would likely leave within months. Her father had been in the military her whole childhood, so she was used to moving around, learning how to fit in, how not to stand out. Perhaps that was why dance was so appealing to her. Moving with others. Being part of something bigger than herself, a language she could speak no matter where she went.

The studios always put her up somewhere until her next gig. Did the transient lifestyle bother her? No, Josie could deal with anything and remain unflustered. Until she could get a regular spot on DNN, she vowed to be single-minded in her focus.

"Yes!" Gabriela replied. "I think the author character is *totally* believable. It's crazy how easy it is for men to break into the literary scene and act like it's their rightful place, isn't it? In Venezuela, it's even worse. Completely male-dominated."

Gabriela was in bed, ensconced under her beautiful high-thread-count sheets with lavender piping to match the pale-purple upholstered headboard. A slim headband pulled her thick, long brown hair off her all-natural, no-enhancements face. From this close up, we could see the laugh lines and crow's feet, her emotions proudly etched on her skin.

"You don't hear about the literary scene in Venezuela too often," I mused.

"I thought the way the protagonist took care of his kids was really well done in the book," Kelly added. "She captured the push-pull of that girlfriend-stepparent role to a tee."

"You think? What are you basing that on?" Josie asked.

"Well, so many of my friends here have gotten divorced and have to deal with new women dating their former spouses," Kelly said. "They complain, but honestly I have so much empathy for them. Could've been us."

"True." Gabriela nodded. "How about we move to the 'lovers' part?"

I took a sip of wine and interjected. "Um, can we pause book club for two seconds?"

"Sure, we spent two minutes discussing the book. That's more than last time," Josie said. "What's new?"

I caught my friends up on my new predicament with Driftwood.
"What?"
"Seriously?"
"Is that even legal?"
"Apparently, yes."

Kelly lifted up her cabernet. "We're gonna need more of this."

"Do you have any ideas you can whip out?" Josie asked. "It doesn't have to be perfect."

"Not really. Who can write a book in, like, a week? No one! But I do have one idea: what about an artist who goes to a Buddhist spa to relax and recharge, but when she lets the handyman enter her room—"

"No, stop there," Josie said. "Too cliché. That's like porn. Plus, what would a handyman even have to fix at a spa? The meditation mats?"

"Fine," I said.

"You could do a sequel to *Poppies*?" Gabriela offered.

"Nope, sequels are usually failures," Kelly said.

"Maybe a historical (haha) novel about a public figure like Cyndi Lauper," I suggested.

"You're right. You have nothing," Josie quipped. "I'm sorry, love, but those ideas are terrible. Any chance your agent could buy you some more time?"

"I don't think so. LeeLee is totally fed up with me, too. And I definitely can't repay the advance without asking Ethan for more from his private accounts, which is demoralizing—and he might say no. I can't stand how money affects the power dynamic between us. I always feel so beholden to him, like I have to beg for everything and he magnanimously says yes sometimes. Totally unpredictable."

"What's in your *heart*? Write that!" Gabriela said.

I rubbed my forehead.

"My kids. That's it. And I won't write about them." I sighed. "This isn't helping. Sorry. I'll think of something."

"Post on Instagram and ask for ideas?" Gabriela tried again.

"Are you kidding? Then my publisher will know I have nothing!"

Kelly adjusted her headband and flipped her white-blonde hair over one shoulder. "Okay, okay. Well, we know you can do it and we love you. How about we go back to the book now for another two minutes? Take your mind off things. How about the school scene at the end?!"

"I know, right?" Josie said.

Kelly quickly added, "And, Pippa, we can talk about it more tomorrow when I land. I can't wait for my LA book event."

"Yes! Can I pick you up at the airport?"

"My publisher got me a car, but thanks."

I raised my eyebrows. "They're really splurging on your tour, huh?"

"Oh no. I'm paying for most of it myself."

"Ah."

"But you'll meet me at the bookstore tomorrow night?"

"Of course!"

I was in no better shape than when book club began. It was all starting to feel hopeless. Why wasn't *this* part of being an author more widely known? Maybe the readers of my first book would be interested to know that the sophomore novel—and all subsequent ones—could be excruciating. That our minds could hold us hostage and work against us. But really, that's not what anyone wanted to read about. Was it?

After leaving the Zoom room, parting with our signature heart emojis and virtual cheers, I picked up the latest Farrow & Ball wallpaper catalog.

My own version of porn.

# Ten

M̶ore broccoli?"

I was serving Max and Zoe dinner after book club. I'd gotten takeout from Farmshop earlier, but reheated it and plated it in a nice dish. Did it really matter *who* steamed the broccoli? I made it look nice and put it on the table next to some roast chicken and potatoes. Clearly indulgences like this would have to end soon if I didn't hand in my book; I could redeploy the family food budget and not have to ask Ethan for more?

"No thanks."

"Nope."

"Just take a little. Both of you."

"Zoe's on her phone," Max said, tattling.

"You know there are no phones at the dinner table," I said, reaching over to try to grab it before Zoe could hide it in her lap.

"*You're* always on your phone, Mom," she said. "Who cares?"

I hated when the kids called me out on this. I really tried hard not to be on my phone so much, but I always came up with excuses. "Instagram is really part of work," I would argue. Or, "I'm not playing Roblox, I'm emailing about my career!" But still. I was on my phone too much. I knew it and they knew it. And yet it was so hard to scale back.

"Not at dinner, though. Never at dinner!"

"Does that really make a difference?" Zoe asked.

"Yes, according to research. This is *family* time."

Zoe threw her phone down like it was a kitchen towel, not a ridiculously overpriced iPhone. I grabbed it and placed it on the kitchen counter.

"By the way," I said, "I forgot to ask. Whatever happened to Todd?"

Zoe waved her hand. "Old news. Over it. Now I like this dude Damien. He's super hot."

"Okaaaaay," I said. "You know it's not just about the outside, it's about—"

"Oh please." Zoe rolled her eyes.

Max wrinkled his nose. "No more boy talk, Zoe. Gross."

"Yeah, let's talk about something else," Zoe said, cutting into her roast chicken.

"Well, I'm having a little problem at work," I said. "Apparently—"

"But, Mom, you don't really *work*," Zoe said. "At least, it doesn't seem like it."

Max smirked while shoveling in his food.

"A writer is always working. Anyway, I found out that if I don't turn in my latest manuscript by Friday at five p.m., my publisher will cancel my contract and demand the advance back. The problem, of course, is that I spent my advance turning the pantry into an office, not to mention on your fifty-seven hoodies, Zoe, and Max's tennis gear."

"Shit," Max said.

"Max!" Zoe and I blurted at the same time.

"Sorry," he said, holding up his hands. "That sucks, Mom. Five p.m. Eastern or Pacific Time?"

"Don't say 'sucks,' please. And I don't think those three hours will make much of a difference, do you?" I said, sighing and spearing a broccoli stalk.

Zoe added, "So what are you going to write about? How are you going to finish it in time? Can Kelly help?"

"Kelly is working on her own book," I said. "I don't know what to do. The last book idea I got really excited about—"

"We know," they said together.

"My editor wants something fresh. But all I can do is stare at the blinking cursor and blank page."

Max put down his fork to grab a sip of water. "Why don't you just submit that?"

"Submit what?" I said, looking up at him.

"Don't chew with your mouth open," Zoe told Max.

"The book. The blank page. A totally blank book. Just say that was the whole point. That you meant for it to be blank. I did that once with my homework. Didn't go over so well, come to think of it."

"Come on, dude," Zoe said. "Let's try to come up with some *real* solutions here."

But as I watched Max slurp his water, the wheels started turning. *Wait a minute. What if I did submit it blank? With nothing in it!* Although, wasn't there a requisite word count in my contract?

I thought back to family trips to the Metropolitan Museum of Art. I remember wondering, "How is this *art*?" Or even, "Come on, I could do that! It's just a few straight lines!"

I didn't *get* that every painting was in dialogue; it was saying something about the artwork that preceded it. It wasn't about how intricate the content was. It was a message, a transformative echo, a call-and-response to what came before. Jackson Pollock's splattered canvases threw out the established norms of figurative painting; the canvas became a receptacle. Mondrian stripped forms down to the minimum. Everyone had a mission and a message that couldn't necessarily be discerned just by looking at a work. Sometimes backstory was the key component. I saw that all the time in the ultra-high-end homes I visited incognito.

*Could I do that with a novel?*

Publishing a blank novel would be a commentary on the literary world. I could say that I was addressing the reader's almost nonexistent attention span. To keep the reader's attention, they'd have to be able to read the words in, well, *no time*. To read *this* book, they wouldn't have to do anything! They could buy it and immediately say they'd read it. Post it on FabulousReads.com. And if it *was* popular, that would be a commentary on the randomness of the industry. It was clever! Or was it stupid? The best ideas were always a mix of both.

"Wait, Max, that's *perfect*," I said.

"Mom, I was kidding."

"No, really," I added, still stewing over the idea. "Or I could just repeat the word 'blank' sixty thousand times."

"I don't know, Mom," Zoe said. "It's kind of like a joke. A social satire. Is that what you want to write?"

I reflected more on the message behind this type of statement piece. Selling a book took a herculean effort from the author: live bookstore events, contributed essays, endless signing. A writer's *writing* job was to produce the actual content before all the marketing and sales, publicity, and celebrity acceptance. Perhaps I didn't even *need* a plot? The book was the story itself! That was fresh! Could this be the original idea I was looking for?

"Mom, do it!" Zoe said. "I'll post about it on social. My friends will go nuts."

"Yeah, it's pretty funny," Max added. "I like it."

"Done! I'm going to do it!" I said, banging my fist on the table. "Yes! I'm doing it!"

I would call the novel *Blank*.

"More potatoes, anyone?"

———

After dinner I padded back to my office. The lights were dim, the sky was black, and my favorite books were winking at me from the bookcase. I could do this!

I opened a new Word document.

*Blank.*

*A Novel. About Nothing.*

*By Pippa Jones.*

It looked great!

I hit Enter till I got to 250 pages, then typed, *The End.*

Then I copied and saved that version and filled it with the word "blank" sixty thousand times over. And then, *The End.*

I emailed them off to my editor, Sidonie, cc'ing my agent, LeeLee.

*Hi, ladies,* I wrote. *I've come up with a completely original idea for my next novel. Two versions attached. Let me know what you think! Xx, Pippa*

Then: swish. Sent.

Could I really pull this off? I didn't have a choice.

# TUESDAY

# Eleven

"What the hell is this?"

"Wait, let me explain."

It was seven in the morning in LA, and LeeLee was calling, panicked, from New York. I was already in the kitchen, cradling the phone between my neck and my shoulder—a habit from the bygone era of landlines, which really did *not* work like cellphones—and braiding Zoe's hair for school as she watched YouTube on her phone. Max was sitting at the kitchen table next to us, finishing his math homework.

"Where is the *book*, Pippa? Where is the work for which Driftwood Publishing paid you? That I negotiated? For which I get a very meager percentage? Is this a joke? Because I'm not laughing. Yesterday you said you were close to finished!"

Max looked up from his assignment.

"Right, but this is even better! Look, LeeLee, I think I've really hit on something. We all know the publishing industry is going through a major period of transition. Sometimes it feels like it doesn't even matter *what's* inside the book. Books that aren't well written sell millions of copies, while heartfelt, beautifully crafted stories literally languish in indie bookstores, rarely dusted off or flipped open unless someone comes in specifically looking for them. Discoverability is next to impossible. Covers have taken on an exaggerated role in bookselling as the primary marketing tool, but how can one image convey an entire book?

The pressure! What even makes a bestseller? I've heard that the bestseller lists are subjective and not even based on actual sales numbers."

"Pippa, while your observations may bear some truth, you can't use that argument to justify not delivering on your contract."

"I *am* delivering on my contract. I sent you a manuscript by the new deadline. It has sixty thousand words. They just all happen to be the same word. The contract didn't specify that it has to be sixty thousand *different* words."

"You can't do this, Pippa. You need to come up with something better. This will end your career."

"Will we still be able to afford Cheerios?" Max asked.

"Shut *up*, Max," said Zoe.

"Guys!!"

"Don't say 'guys'!" Zoe added.

"Pippa," LeeLee said, "are you listening to me?"

"Yes, of course. I'm also with my kids. But yes."

I could feel her rolling her eyes. LeeLee didn't want—or even like—kids.

"I swear, Pippa, if you don't submit a real version, I can't keep you on as a client."

"What? I've been your client for twelve years!"

"Yes. When you were *writing*—not performing literary stunts like this."

I put down Zoe's hairbrush and grabbed the phone off my shoulder.

"It isn't a literary stunt," I said carefully. "It's art. It's a reflection on the state of publishing today. It's a signpost that things are not as they should be, that we can and should make changes. It's holding up a mirror to consumption patterns that don't follow logic. And, I think it's funny!"

"It's not funny," LeeLee retorted. "And you better explain this to Sidonie before she calls me, because I will not defend you. I'm telling you, Pippa. I can't stand behind you on this."

"Well, LeeLee, you also didn't stand behind me yesterday when Driftwood came out of the blue and said they might have to reclaim my advance. Isn't it your job as my literary agent to protect me? To help me?"

"It is. Or it was. But when you have a contract to write a book, you have to write a book. Even your kids can understand that."

"Ouch," Zoe said, clearly eavesdropping.

"I did write a book. I was almost done with *Podlusters*. And it was good! But then—"

"Enough with *Podlusters*! I know it was unfortunate, but you're a writer. You must have more than one idea."

Ethan wandered in wearing pajama pants and a wrinkled LA Rams T-shirt. Up early today, apparently. I rolled my eyes.

"What's going on?" he asked.

I turned back to the phone.

"Look, I love this idea," I said. "And so will many other authors and readers. This will be a sensation, a movement, and you'll see how wrong you were."

Okay, maybe I was getting carried away. It could be a terrible idea. I could lose my contract, have to repay my advance, ruin my life . . .

"LeeLee, hold on for two seconds," I said. "Just two seconds."

I pressed Mute and put the phone on the table, then covered my face with my hands. Was this a huge mistake? Did I really believe this would work? Or would I become a total laughingstock and never write professionally again? I could get canceled. Torn apart on Twitter. Destroyed. And then what? Ethan wasn't earning much. His savings would eventually run out. Maybe we'd have to leave our home, find a public school somewhere in a less expensive neighborhood. Maybe we'd even have to move to . . . the Valley.

I moaned.

"Mom, it's going to be okay," Max said. "If you think it's a good idea, it's a good idea."

I nodded behind my hands, trying to hold back tears.

"Yeah, it's okay, Mom," Zoe said, joining Max for a group hug. "Now go tell LeeLee she's the luckiest agent around."

We all hugged tightly.

"You are the sweetest things," I said. "Sometimes."

We laughed. This. *This* was what mattered. We'd be okay no matter what.

With newfound determination, I picked up the phone.

"I'm back. And I'm sure *Blank* is going to be a huge hit. You're going to be thanking me for years."

"At least you seem to have found your confidence again," LeeLee snarled. "But I have to disagree. This little stunt of yours will be a giant failure. And I want no part of it. Good luck, Pippa. Don't come begging me to come back when you've destroyed your reputation and ended your career."

"Jeez, LeeLee. I didn't think you were such a fair-weather friend. But fine. Have a nice life."

I pressed End. It wasn't half as satisfying as slamming down a headset into a receiver, but it still gave me a sense of power.

"Bitch!" I said to the phone.

"Go, Mom!" Max said, high-fiving me.

"Sorry for cursing," I said.

"That was pretty badass," Zoe said, smiling. "Loved seeing you stand up for yourself and not succumb to the patriarchy."

"Zoe, do you even know what 'the patriarchy' means? I'm a woman who just got fired by another woman."

"But a woman from a big company run by a man, right?"

"Ugh," I said, rolling my eyes. "Whatever."

I turned to Ethan, who was drinking a double espresso and rubbing his eyes.

"I just got fired by my agent. But my book is going to be a bestseller."

"Nice," Ethan said. "More turmeric lattes."

# Twelve

D arling? How *are* you? Ethan just called and told me you'd gone crazy."

I'd walked in from an open house and a call with Zoe's guidance counselor, the car still humming in shutdown mode in the garage, always worrying me that I would somehow get carbon monoxide poisoning. I was clad in a 1950s swing skirt and tight cardigan, my costume du jour. I'd just popped into a six-bedroom in Bel Air that a famous actor was trying to sell. I'd gotten the best shot of his cat's custom-made bed, which simply said "Pussy Pad." Insta-gold. I already had 14K likes by the time I got home—and an offer to be a spokesperson for Pussy. I mean, really.

"Oh, hi, Mom."

"Actually, he told me you'd gone *batshit* crazy, which I chuckled at. Didn't I, Seymour?"

"You sure did," Seymour said in the background.

"Seymour, do bats even shit?"

"Course they do! It's white."

"What's white, dear?"

Seymour was undoubtedly in a lounge chair by the pool in Palm Springs. My mom's second husband was the ultimate yes-man. Perhaps bisexual. There was a bevy of gorgeous young men in tight bathing suits surrounding them at all times, chihuahuas circling the brigade. But none of that seemed to bother her.

"Mom, please. *You* called *me*?"

"Oh. Yes. So I did."

I headed upstairs to put on workout clothes. Of course nothing would fit right, per usual. Three skirts and two tops, one of which was from my High Holidays section of the closet, were strewn inside out on the wood floor from earlier that day, an ode to this particular stage of my metabolism. It would have to be another heavily accessorized outfit. I should just open a store called Flash and sell big necklaces, reading glasses, elastic-waist skirts, and long-sleeve dresses. Oh, and towels.

"So what's going on, Pippa? Is it true that you've lost your mind?"

"No, I'm fine," I said, grabbing leggings from the drawer. Wait, weren't these Zoe's? "I'm getting dressed for a hike with Kelly, who just got to town. And I'm *not* going crazy. I've made a business decision for my next book that not everyone is loving. And then that fair-weather agent LeeLee fired me."

"No! How dare she? That little witch."

"Who?!" I heard Seymour ask.

"Pippa's agent!"

"I know, Mom. It wasn't cool at all."

"I'm going to call her myself."

"Please don't."

I could imagine my mother huffing around their modern house in a silk floor-length robe, drink in hand. She'd sold our childhood home in Pasadena after I went off to Bluestone for college. It was time for her to move on after my dad died. He was twenty years older than she was (they met when she was a waitress and he spilled wine everywhere) and passed away when I was too young to remember. My mom would recount that he had raspy breath from years of smoking and that he always brandished coins from behind my ears, like Penn & Teller. Apparently it was a "blessing" of a death because he didn't suffer long: only three months from diagnosis to his last day.

My mom kept his clothes in the closet, his shoes beside hers, until she met Seymour ten years later, when I was in middle school. I used to try on his shoes and clomp around their bedroom. My dad had been a book lover, too. Mom told me—and I saw a few yellow-hued square photos to prove it—that his favorite pastime was sitting in his armchair, sighing as he read, after managing the local hardware store all day. Part of me always had him in mind when I wrote. What would *he* think of *Blank*? I could see him chuckling, but also putting his head in his hands, looking defeated. I was definitely having some doubts about the whole thing, but I was already in too deep to back out. I just shoved down those negative thoughts.

"Now, what *is* the idea for your book, darling? Come on. Spill it. I don't have all day."

How was my mom busier than me?

"Okay. It's called *Blank*. It's a book that repeats the word 'blank' sixty thousand times. Or I might just leave the pages totally blank. I'm not sure yet. I sent in both versions. I think it's a really clever idea, a reflection on the state of the publishing industry and the randomness of success. You know, like art."

Silence.

"Mom?"

More silence.

"Mom? You there?"

I looked down at the phone and shook it.

And then, a slow cackle.

"Ha! P*ippa*! That's hil*arious*. Seymour, listen to this! Pippa's going to try to sell an empty book. Like the Emperor's New Clothes!"

"She's writing a book about clothes? What does *she* know about fashion?"

"No, Seymour . . ." I sighed while she repeated herself. Then she turned back to me. "Okay, that's very funny, darling, but it is *not* a good idea for a book. What will people think who spend money on it and get . . . nothing?"

"They won't get *nothing*. They'll get to have a voice in the publishing world."

"Not really, though, riiiiight? Pippa, dear. *No one* cares about the publishing world except you. Certainly not readers. They just want to be fed great books—and to be told which books are great and which aren't. Don't waste your time with this. You're supposed to be a WRITER. You're supposed to WRITE! This book is like a gag gift. You're so gifted with words. They just flow off the page when you write. Can't you come up with something else? *Any*thing?"

"Well, *I* love the idea. People will feel like they've purchased a piece of art. It will become famous and more valuable over time. Like an NFT."

"A what?"

"A non-fungible token."

"Like a subway token?"

"Never mind. Bad analogy. Like a limited-edition pocketbook."

"Ah." She sighed. "Look, dear. *Beg* LeeLee to take you back and tell her you made a mistake. And then tell Ethan to take you somewhere to clear your head. Perhaps a night in Laguna. And make yourself an extra-strong drink."

"Mom, it's not even noon."

"So?"

I shook my head.

Mom switched tacks. "What do your writer friends think about this?"

"I haven't told them yet."

"Well, what are you waiting for?"

"For you to get off the phone, for starters."

She chuckled.

"Next time I call you, I won't even say hello!" she said. "It'll be a *blank* phone call!"

"So not funny."

"A blank email! A blank newspaper!" She was laughing hysterically.

"Mom!"

Okay, this probably wasn't good. My mom was making fun of me. I'd been fired by my agent. Ethan thought I'd lost my mind. Only the kids were supporting me. Was I right that *Blank* would be a hit?

Or was this about to be the biggest disaster of my life?

# Thirteen

"How are you always so *chill*?"

We were taking a walk around the Silver Lake Reservoir before Kelly's paperback launch. She needed to *clear her lungs* after the long flight. The drive to Silver Lake from my neighborhood was like driving from Midtown Manhattan to Greenwich, Connecticut, but in LA that was totally normal for an errand, coffee, or hike.

"I'm not always so chill," Kelly said. "Are you kidding? My parents call me all the time, still hoping I'll change my mind and become a lawyer or a doctor, not someone who sits around and makes up stories about fighting all day."

"So crazy," I said. "We're in our forties. Will our parents ever stop pestering us?"

"Nope. Never. Comes with the job description. We'll probably do it to our kids, too."

"Shoot me if I do," I muttered.

"Remind me again why we're walking in circles?"

"This is what we do here in LA, Kelly," I said. "We don't sit. We walk outside and talk. We call it *hiking*. Or we play tennis, pickleball, beach volleyball. Get with the program. You remember. You lived here once when we were young and fit."

"I mean, I walk the reservoir in New York three times a week, but it just feels more intentional, maybe because there are so many people doing it with me. This loop feels way too rustic for me and we're the only ones out here."

"Just walk."

But then I stopped for a second.

"Actually, speaking of feeling like the only ones, what's the latest with Gaby these days? Have you spoken to her? I feel like she's been a little distant lately."

"I think she's the *opposite* of distant with her new trainer," Kelly responded.

"Oh right. I have to say, she's really managed to pull off this non-monogamy situation. Did you see this coming?! She was the last person I'd have predicted would pal around with the hottest guys while married. And how come her kids never figure things out?"

"Maybe they know?"

"Maybe . . ."

We kept walking.

I glanced over at Kelly, her ponytail bopping on her faded Patagonia fleece. "So what do you think about it—about fidelity in general? Do we all just accept that Gabriela cheats?"

"Gabriela and Juan Carlos have an arrangement. He cheats, too," Kelly said. "So it's not even *cheating*, is it? If they both know? How could *we* not accept it if they do? Plus, when they're together, they're always really kind, considerate, and loving to each other. Maybe they're the ones getting it right."

"I know, but it still just feels wrong to me. She should leave him if she doesn't love him."

"I think she does love him. I think they have a good partnership going. And I think it's really up to each couple to figure out how to get through life together. Plus, leaving someone isn't that easy. Sometimes it takes being with someone new to realize how wrong the person you're with really is. For Gabriela, it seems like Juan Carlos isn't *wrong*. He's just not *everything*. They've figured out an arrangement that makes them both happy."

"Something you want to share, Kelly?" I asked. "You're arguing pretty strongly for this . . . arrangement. How are things with Arthur?"

"Fine, fine. You know. Fine." She sighed and quickly checked her phone.

"Sounds exciting."

"Exciting it is *not*. But after almost fifteen years, we're good. Fine. He's still the person I want to tell all the latest and greatest to. He's still trying to be a good dad; he's just very formal. You know—a bit stiff."

"Stiff can be good," I said.

"You and the sex jokes."

"Oh, come on. They're so infrequent."

Kelly grinned. "The jokes or the sex?"

"Both." I laughed out loud. Then I had to ask, "But you wouldn't cheat on him?"

Kelly looked at her feet. Her lack of response hung in the air.

"Stop," she said, finally. "How are you, anyway? How are Max and Zoe?"

"They're great! Well, you saw Max. He's so sweet. Really into chess these days. Trying to learn his haftorah portion without much success. And Zoe's . . . Zoe. She's into some senior named Damien, but apparently it's over with her boyfriend, Todd, or maybe he wasn't her boyfriend. Always drama. Always something. The kids are a real handful. But I adore them. You know, when I don't want to strangle them. They're everything to me."

"I hear that. Hey, did you see that Rachel Wegman got a divorce?"

"Rachel Wegman from college? The one who married the founder of that toilet app from *Shark Tank*?"

"Yep, her. He was cheating on her all over town. Everyone else knew."

"Oh boy. They looked so perfect together. Always in their beautiful hunting or fishing outfits with their Cavalier King Charles spaniels, like they lived in the pages of *Town & Country*."

"You never really know what goes on in anyone else's relationship," Kelly said.

"Very true," I added. "Very, very true."

"All good with you and Ethan?"

"Oh, you know. We're kind of . . . drifting apart."

"Aren't we all?"

Usually I could stomach the thought of my marriage not being what the storybooks predicted. There was no Prince Charming in my life and that was . . . fine. I mean, really. How many super-happy marriages were there anyway? Maybe mine was better than most? But sometimes, when I really let myself go there, I wondered if *maybe* I would consider doing something about it. Could there possibly be a happier life out there waiting for me? Ha! Forget it. Who was I kidding. I'd learned to . . . settle. And I'd have to be okay with that. For eternity. Jeez.

"We're fine. I think we're probably just as happy as most couples. Right?"

"Sure," Kelly said.

But neither of us sounded too convinced.

# Fourteen

The courtyard at Bookends Bookshop was packed even though it was in the fifties, a *very* chilly evening in LA. Kelly was doing a reading and Q&A about the paperback version of her latest thriller *HighJILLed*, a holiday suspense story in which the main protagonist, Angie, is on a plane that's hijacked by a woman named Jill—and then Angie gets the courage to use her martial arts moves and chokes Jill out, saving the day. There was more to it, naturally. But Kelly could explain. Of *course*, I would be there and would post about it (#womensupportingwomen #authorssupportingauthors #friendship #highjilled).

I was a little late; I'd brought Max with me at the last minute, bribing him with a stop at Sweet Daisy for ice cream. I had the vegan dark chocolate flavor. You know, to be healthy. We arrived when Kelly was just starting to read at the podium outside the famous indie bookstore.

I scanned the crowd and waved to the dozen authors I recognized. The literary scene in Los Angeles was quite small.

"How do you know all of them again?" Max asked.

"Oh, honey. When you work in words, you need all the help you can get."

"Can I go inside and buy a book?"

"Sure, but try to buy paperbacks."

"Why?"

"Because it's the exact same story, only cheaper. It's why we fly coach."

"Mom, we don't fly coach."

"Well, it's why we *buy* coach and have your uncle Brad use his miles to upgrade us."

"Got it."

I tiptoed into the crowd and settled in next to a group of novelists. We blew kisses and went back to listening to the origin story of Kelly's book (a turbulent flight, a powerful flight attendant, a what-if scenario). At least we could all be there to support her, smile, wave, and clap while wrapping our fleeces tightly around us. Book events were a crapshoot and we all knew it. Sometimes they were mobbed; other times they were vacant. At one of my *Poppies* events, only three people showed up—and one of them was the store employee tasked with filming. Kelly had a full courtyard.

Once Kelly had answered the last question ("What is your process like?"), we all burst into conversation as if we *hadn't* just seen each other last week at Will Bernstein's book launch for *The History of the Riviera Club*. At least I'd managed to get a fantastic snapshot of a three-bed-room Beverly Hills bungalow on the way home from *that* event. The home had a stash of old-school *Playboys* next to the toilet. As Zoe would say: cringe. Even my Instagram followers responded with a series of disgusted emojis.

As our little group ambled over to the bookstore entrance, I decided to conduct an ad hoc focus group.

"Okay, question. What do you all think about this concept? My next novel is only going to have the word 'blank' repeated sixty thousand times so I abide by my contract yet make a point about the book industry. Or maybe it'll be completely blank inside. I have both versions. If I make it a bestseller, it will be the perfect commentary on the industry. How it doesn't even matter what we write; it's mostly name value and marketing. People might buy it just because they loved my first book without even knowing what it's about. I'm calling it *Blank*."

"Is this a joke or for real?" Will asked.

"Not a joke."

They all glanced at each other. Silence and slow nodding. I could see them trying to decide what to say.

Ada, the rom-com queen (bestselling author of *Twerk Your Heart Out*), pursed her lips, looking up at the sky as if thinking *really* hard. "I love it."

"It's pretty hilarious," Will added, nodding. "Does it even matter what we write? But you have to have a blurb on the front cover from, like, Obama."

"Yes!" I exclaimed. "Love that. 'Obama says: This is the book of the year *not* to read.'"

"Hmm, I'm not so sure that's going to work," said Maeve, the literary novelist turned screenwriter. "Won't people want to get what they're paying for? A story? An escape? Ten hours when they don't have to make decisions or email or talk to anyone?"

"Come on," I said. "Does anyone *really* finish a book anymore—and does it matter? I feel like most people fake it. They just nod when people talk about the books they're reading, like, 'Oh yes, wasn't that great?' And honestly I don't blame them. It's not their fault. There are eight million other things competing for their attention. Phones have short-circuited our brains. I can't even get my kids to watch a *movie*. Or even a TV show. It's, like, so old school. If it's not on TikTok or YouTube, it's like it doesn't exist."

"Oh my gosh," Ada said, hands slapped over her mouth, looking at us in horror. "What if people *stop reading*?"

"They won't stop reading, Ada," Maeve said. "People *need* an escape from their lives. And books have been around forever. *A tale as old as time.*"

"See? That was from a movie," I said.

"Both. A book-to-film adaptation," Maeve said.

I continued: "Imagine someone just came up with the idea of reading. Like, 'Hey, let's launch a product with no pictures, just words and letters. To enjoy it, you have to sit in one place and stare at it for hours, and then the whole story will slowly unfold *just to you inside your brain*. It might take you months to find out what happens in the end. It's a completely solitary endeavor and you can't do *anything else* at the same time. Oh, and you need to purchase it up front, hoping you'll like it. But if you don't, there's no refund. Sorry! And there are literally millions of other products that look basically identical—some are great and some are terrible, and there's almost no way to know ahead of time. Good luck. Go spend thirty dollars!'"

I'd stunned our group into silence.

"Yikes," Will said.

"So maybe *Blank* will make readers feel *good* because they can actually cross 'reading a book' off their lists and move it off their nightstands before it can collect dust. Everyone wants to be a part of a movement. Everyone wants to connect. If enough people 'read' *Blank* and discuss it, it will create that sense of connection. That's what books are supposed to do: connect readers to authors. Readers to each other. That's why book clubs are so popular! It's like that mural on Montana: 'Stories are best when shared.'"

"Right, but they still won't get a story to read," Maeve countered.

"No. It's more like a coffee table book. People buy those all the time, and they mostly just sit there and look pretty. And *Blank* will be much smaller and less expensive."

"I read my coffee table books," Kelly remarked in passing. She was on her way to sign books.

"You do?" Ada asked her. "Does that count as reading?"

"Of course," I said.

Ada turned to me. "Could *Blank* be used as a journal?"

"Hmm. Maybe. Or we could also make *Blank: A Journal*. A companion piece. That would be great. But for now, it's just supposed to get people talking, thinking, bonding, connecting. All the things a good book should do."

"Except usually books involve *reading*," Ada said.

"Well, there's that," I admitted.

"They can read the blurbs," Maeve added. "And the back cover copy."

"And all the horrific reviews that will surely come," Kelly added from her signing table.

*"Rude,"* I called back.

"Well, I think it's amazing," said Will. "Show everyone that what makes something a bestseller these days is all about packaging and branding, not only the content."

"I don't know, Pippa. I'd be careful," Ada said. "This just might blow up in your face."

"I'm aware," I said. "It might. But I don't have another book ready and my due date has long passed. So if I don't want to be in breach of contract, I have to try. Will you support me? Show up to my book signings? Provide me with blurbs?"

Will, Ada, Kelly, and Maeve all looked at one another, and with a universal shrug said yes. A few hangers-on looked down awkwardly.

"I'm not so sure about this, Pippa," Jane chimed in from Kelly's signing line. She was always a Negative Nelly. "I think this could be career suicide. What about the rest of us who are still working tirelessly on our books? Doesn't this undermine our hard work?"

"No, not at all! I want it to draw *more* attention to your hard work by illuminating the industry's foibles!"

"I guess we'll just have to see, then," Jane said. "Is your publisher willing to print it?"

"About that . . . I'm still waiting to hear. It's been almost twenty-four hours, and crickets. My agent isn't exactly enthused, but I haven't heard from the publisher." (I left out the bit about LeeLee firing me.)

Max walked over with a shopping bag full of books.

"I thought I said one paperback!"

"You didn't say that. You said 'paperbacks.' No limit."

"You bought ten books."

"I know. I thought you liked supporting bookstores?"

"If he'd bought ten hardcovers, you could've just gotten him, like, a couch," Will said.

"Maybe not a couch," Maeve added. "But definitely an ottoman."

"What'd you get, Max?" Ada asked, peeking into his bag. "Any of mine?"

Max blushed.

"I'm not quite old enough for your books," he said.

"Oh, buddy, I think you are," Will added, swinging his arm around Max's shoulders and leading him back to the store with a wink at me.

"Hi, ladies."

Ethan. What was he doing here?!

"Ethan! Shouldn't you be off producing a play or something?" Kelly said, getting up from her signing station to give him a hug.

Ada and Maeve followed. "Hi, Ethan," they said.

Ethan waved hello. "It's the writing crew of Los Angeles, single-handedly keeping the literary spirit alive!"

"Funny," I said.

"Always a charmer, Ethan," Kelly said.

"Seriously. What are you doing here?" I asked again.

"Come on! I heard there was a book party. I didn't want to miss it."

I raised my eyebrows, waiting for the truth. "I thought you were working."

"I need a new book—research for the show—and saw on the cal-endar that you'd be here, so I figured, why not? Plus, how could I miss Kelly's big moment? We've had to deal with her talking about this book for long enough."

"Come on, Ethan," Kelly said. "Let's go find you some of my books to buy."

It was so strange that Ethan showed up, but that was Ethan. Completely unpredictable and occasionally quite charming. Why was

I even surprised? At least my writing friends seemed to get my idea. If they'd all hated it, I might've had to pivot before it was too late. But no! Support! Encouragement! Or did they secretly want to watch me fall flat on my face? Well, I was going to keep selling the concept, absolute certainty in my voice.

If I didn't believe in it, no one else would either.

# WEDNESDAY

# Fifteen

**M**ichael wants you to come in to the office to discuss. He's in LA. Does 10:30 a.m. work?

I was still reading emails in bed, about to wake up Zoe and Max, when I got the text from my editor, Sidonie. One of the occupational hazards of working in LA is always waking up three hours behind. New York is the center of the publishing world. We're just film adjacent on the West Coast.

Michael . . . as in, the head honcho of Driftwood? I wrote back.

Yep.

I'd only met Michael Bostwick once or twice, at large industry events. He'd basically looked through me on his way to someone more important. Even after *Poppies* became a bestseller and then a movie— nothing. Now, a meeting?

This can't be good. I'll be there.

Will LeeLee be coming with you? Driftwood couldn't get ahold of her by phone or email. That's why they called me.

*Guess I forgot to tell Sidonie about the whole my-agent-dumped-me thing.*

Actually, I typed, LeeLee and I have parted ways.

Three dots, then . . . nothing.

Is Michael pissed? I wrote.

Pissed is not exactly the right word.

Oh boy.

————

I managed to catch Josie between segments for a quick SOS text exchange. I was brushing my teeth and kept dripping toothpaste on my iPhone screen.

The head of Driftwood wants to meet with me this morning. In person.

That guy Michael?!

Yep. You know him?

A little. Is that a good or bad sign?

Probably terrible. He's never even said hello to me.

Where are you meeting?

Driftwood's LA office.

Yikes.

Yeah. I sat and stared at the screen for a few seconds, waiting for Josie to reply, but she didn't. Have you ever met the CEO of your company?

He wouldn't know who I was if I slammed into his windshield.

Lovely image.

Good luck.

Xxoo

I grabbed my cozy robe off the bathroom hook and glanced over at Ethan, still sound asleep.

"Drifting apart" sounded so passive, I thought. Ethan and I weren't drift-*ing*. We'd drift-*ed*. We might as well be on opposite coasts, and I wasn't sure I even wanted to meet again. He had cleaved us apart with an ice pick long ago. Literally apart. He wouldn't touch me.

It wasn't like I was tempted by other men. I seemed to have no sex drive at all. Ethan apparently felt the same. At least I hoped so—he certainly was touchy at the book event with all my literary lady friends. Was this what the rest of our lives would be like? Silently resentful coexistence with the occasional one-sided fondle?

The first few years we were together, Ethan was the golden child. Everywhere we went, fans asked for his autograph. But as time marched on, people stopped recognizing him as "that famous middle-school kid." He could pump gas *without* ending up in *Us Weekly*—not that he ever pumped his own gas. His irrelevance seemed to filter into his self-perception and, by proxy, his attitude toward me.

If *he* wasn't important anymore, surely *I* wouldn't find him appealing, so why should he even try? I wish I didn't still find him physically attractive, but I did.

When *Poppies* became a hit, Ethan was even less excited to be with me, his own star permanently eclipsed by his previously unthreatening wife. His pivot into the theater world was mostly in name. He had yet to make inroads, especially since the real center of that world was in New York. How could I play a key role in his midlife narrative? And did I want to? Would he stray to find an *actual* supporting actress? Did I care? I wasn't so sure. Look how happy Gabriela and Juan Carlos were with their untraditional arrangement, whereas lately Ethan and I were constantly bickering, snapping at each other, angry. And I really did want Ethan to be happy and feel loved. What if I wasn't the best person for him either? Didn't the father of my kids deserve to have real love? Who even knew. Maybe I was losing it. Everything was fine. *This is just what marriage is like in the long term . . . I think?*

Plus, we barely saw each other. Most nights I was in REM sleep by the time he got into bed. During the days, we'd pass like ships in the night. Meetings, calls, kids, meals. No real connection. "It is what it is," my mom would say. But still.

I tromped up the stairs, but the kids weren't in their rooms. A miracle! Were they already dressed and ready for school?

"Kids?"

I headed back down and found Max and Zoe in the kitchen, their heads hunched over bowls of Honey Nut Cheerios. Turned out they could pour from a cereal box themselves! Milk, too—another miracle! I wrapped my blue bathrobe tightly around my waist, noticing that there wasn't much slack anymore. I had my reading glasses on my head, my bare feet chilly on the reclaimed-wood floor.

"Hi, loves," I said, kissing each of them on the head. Both of them barely reacted. "Um, hello? Guys?" I waved my hand in front of their faces.

"Hey Mom," Max said without looking up. "Can I have some chocolate chip pancakes?"

"Sure, can I make a cup of coffee first?"

He seemed to consider this question. Then nodded. "Okay."

I shook my head, grabbed my favorite "I'd Rather Be Reading" mug, and popped in a coffee pod.

"Anything important at school today, anyone?"

"The usual," Max said. "Chess after, remember? Aren't you taking me?"

"Yes! Right. Of course. Zoe? Remind me of your after-school stuff today."

"Aren't you the one who's supposed to be reminding me?"

"Aren't you the one who's almost old enough to drive?"

"O-kaaaay. Well, I'm going to this guy Damien's today."

"Damien, the hot guy?"

My phone dinged.

"Wait, hold that thought. I want to hear about Damien."

A text from Brittany.

What's all this I hear about a book with no words? What kind of crazy shit is that?

It was followed by a GIF of a sailboat about to capsize in a storm.

It's going to be great! I texted back.

Not everybody around here is so sure about that, she wrote.

I'm committed.

Oh you will be.

Hahaha.

I was screwed.

"Time to get ready for school, people. Let's do this. I have a big day ahead. And, Zoe, show me a picture of Damien?"

"Not a chance."

# Sixteen

T"ell us, Pippa. What makes you think this book has *commercial* appeal?"

I was in the conference room at Driftwood's Century City office. Floor-to-ceiling windows revealed an unobstructed view of Beverly Hills. Michael, the publisher and CEO, a silver-haired former collegiate wrestler with product-filled curls, full lips, a deep tan, and an angular jaw, sat at the head of the table wearing jeans, a white V-neck, and a blazer (i.e., LA casual). He was flanked by two young female assistants with slicked-back ponytails, a senior editor I vaguely recognized from a script-writing class, the head of marketing who had just come over from Mayer Brothers, a lawyer I'd never seen, and the publicity chief, who had recently saved the career of an imprisoned author. They were pulling out all the stops.

"Do *you* think it's a commercial idea?" I threw back.

Michael leaned forward and stared at me intently. Everyone held their breath and waited for him to speak.

"No," he said, settling back in this chair. "No, I don't. Not at all. I think you're making a mockery out of our esteemed publishing house. Driftwood has been around for eighty-five years. We don't sell books and deliver nothing. In fact, we're actively contemplating a lawsuit against you if you go ahead with this. Aren't we, Rodger?"

"We are," the lawyer said.

"So tell us. Why do you think *Blank* is a good idea?"

I took a deep breath and stood up. I had nothing to lose. I started walking around the table to make my case.

"Okay, I know it's unconventional. But here's the thing. These days, it seems like all the good ideas are taken. There are so many books flooding the marketplace that it's hard to get *any* of them to stand out. Fantastic books go unrecognized, while others randomly sell millions. It's often arbitrary. And what about *the readers*? They're being inundated with options, with *no* curation. Just walking into a bookstore is overwhelming—not to mention scrolling through websites—and selecting a book is close to impossible. There are so many options that readers simply take what we or celebrities feed them. That's not showing them any respect. We can and must do better. We need to respect authors' work and readers' intellect.

"By publishing *Blank*, Driftwood would be showing solidarity and compassion for readers and authors. It would be acknowledging what other publishers are ignoring. What if *Blank* does really well? That would just prove my point! It almost doesn't matter what's *inside* books anymore. It's all about the buzz. The name of the author. The hype around it. TikTok readers crying about it. Readers now *must* judge a book by its cover. And even if this book *doesn't* do well, at least it will give publicists and reporters something to cover. And it'll position me better for my next book."

Michael laughed out loud. "Ha! Next book? You're awfully presumptuous."

I walked toward Michael's seat as he swiveled around.

"But what if I'm *right*? I think people will buy it in droves. And if Driftwood doesn't want to publish it, I know I'll find someone else who will."

Silence in the boardroom.

Everyone stared down at their hands.

I waited for Michael to tell me I was done. Over. That my contract was canceled. That *I* was canceled.

He slowly lifted himself out of his chair—he towered over me—then looked me straight in the eye. His eyes were gorgeous actually. Wait, stop. Was Michael *hot*? I could feel my face flush as everyone held their breath.

Michael seemed to be taking it all in. Then, he smiled. A huge, wide, warm smile with perfect teeth. Who was his dentist?

"Course correction," he said. "I'm backing this horse."

Wait, had I heard correctly? Was *I* the horse in this scenario?

"Pippa, I think you just sold me. I get it. And I think readers will get it, too. It'll spark conversation. It'll *mean* something."

"*Yes!* Exactly. Thank you. Thanks, Michael. I promise. It'll be great. Really."

And just like that, everyone in the room was on my side.

"Great idea!"

"Brilliant!"

"Fabulous!"

The townspeople had just been waiting to take their cue from the emperor.

"Just don't mess this up," he said to me, quietly.

Then Michael addressed the team.

"Alright. Here's what we can do. We'll launch a big campaign to promote the book, throw all our publicity might behind it, all of it. But you have to earn out your advance and sell as many copies as we based your up-front payment on. In this case . . . can someone look up how many copies that would be?"

Silence. Typing. Everyone looking at their screens.

"One hundred thousand copies," an intern said.

"Paperback or hardcover?" Michael barked.

"Hardcover."

Michael whistled. "That's going to be tough. Okay. You sell a hundred thousand copies of this sketchbook and we're good. If you sell any less, you have to repay the difference of whatever you owe us. If you sell ninety thousand, you pay us back for the other ten thousand. Understand?"

I nodded.

"And if you don't sell a hundred thousand, don't think you'll ever get a book deal with us again."

I gulped.

*Oh boy.*

This was becoming very, very real. Could I do it? One hundred thousand copies? *That's insane!* Ninety-five percent of books don't sell five thousand copies. Everyone in the room was looking at me. Michael's eyebrows were raised, expectant. Brittany was shaking her head and giving me an "eek" expression.

The silence felt tangible.

"I'm in," I said triumphantly, my hands not so ironically on my hips.

A few people clapped meekly only to receive glares and quickly shove their hands back under the table.

"Okay. Then we're in. We'll make *Blank* our lead summer title. We'll rush production in time for beach-read season. Pitch all national media. Start organizing a multicity book tour. Let's roll out the red carpet for this one. Operation Bestseller. Works every time."

"What's Operation Bestseller?" I asked.

Michael just smirked. "We know exactly how to make a book hit the bestseller list. It's just a matter of which one we decide to push. And, Pippa, today is your book's lucky day."

See?! This was what drove me nuts! He'd literally picked my book to be a bestseller! I *knew* the publishing system was somewhat rigged. It was infuriating that select executives could just decide which books would hit the list, without reader feedback and when countless other authors were biting their fingernails, hoping and praying their books would break out. It was almost predecided.

"Great," I said. "And you'll share all the publishing secrets along the way?"

"Yeah right," Michael said. "You better get to work on an actual book. If this takes off, we'll need another book—a *real* book—ready to go. One that isn't a joke."

"Got it."

"Okay, team. Does everyone understand? Publication month will be June. Let's say June fourteenth. Is that a Tuesday? Can someone in production confirm that it works?"

"Uh, Michael?" an assistant said. "There's almost no way—"

"Great," Michael responded.

The managing editor nodded nervously, scribbling notes.

"Get on this, people. Top priority. Pippa," Michael said, walking toward the door. He looked back at me with those steel-blue eyes. "I want to manage this launch myself. You and I can work closely on it. Jessica, give Pippa my cell, will you?"

Jessica, ponytail girl #1, nodded and then glared at me. I took out my phone to divert my gaze. She scared me a little.

Michael paused on his way out, his hand gripping the doorframe. He looked into the sea of people, nodding his head for dramatic effect.

"Let's do this."

Why did I notice that he wasn't wearing a ring?

The door shut behind him, and the rest of us just sat around the table for a minute, stupefied. Then everyone bolted up and started shouting directions.

Maybe my unwritten book would make me a writer again?

# THURSDAY

# Seventeen

"Phone!"

"What? What's going on?!"

Ethan started shoving me.

"The phone! Get the phone."

I turned on the bedside light while my sleepy brain caught up: The phone was ringing in the middle of the night. That wasn't good.

"Hello?"

"Pippa, it's me."

"Kelly? Are you okay?"

"Sorry, didn't mean to freak you out. Just go on Twitter."

"Kelly, you're calling me in the middle of the night about a tweet? You almost gave me a heart attack!"

"Sorry. Sorry. It's the morning in New York. I forgot about the time difference."

"Hold on, I'm finding my glasses."

"If you lived on the East Coast, I wouldn't have woken you up."

"Ah, the one perk."

Ethan nudged me again. "What's going on?"

"It's all good. It's just Kelly."

"Lovely," I heard her say. "Can't you pretend it's exciting to hear from me?"

"Why is she calling?" he asked.

"Send him my love," she said.

Ethan overheard and nodded.

"Your *love*? It's too early in the morning for your sarcastic humor," I said. "My brain can't even process it."

I opened Twitter. And saw 10,237 comments on an anonymous tweet: One-time literary sensation @pippajonesauthor is faking her next book—and ruining her career. Blank? No thank you.

"Oh noooooooooooo."

"What? Now what's going on?" Ethan asked.

"There's a tweet going viral about me. And *Blank*. Crap!"

"I warned you about this," he said, turning away from me. "You made your bed. Now you have to sleep in it."

"Brilliant analogy. Thanks. And you sleep in that bed, too, remember? You're literally in it right now." I turned back to the phone. "I can't believe this. Kelly, who even tweeted this?"

"It's anonymous—I don't know," she said. "Didn't you *just* have your big publishing meeting yesterday? Sounds like someone there wasn't a fan."

I tried to remember who was in the room. The intern?

I scrolled through the comments. There was a hideous picture of me from Kelly's Bookends event in which I was giving Max cash to buy books, but you couldn't see Max and it looked like I was trying to bribe someone in the bookstore. Caption: *Paying to play, Pippa?*

I moaned, covering my eyes. Then I lifted the phone back up and put Kelly on speaker.

"Listen to this comment," I said. "'If Pippa had just remained a has-been, it would've been fine. But by publishing a blank book, she's not only stirring the pot; she's also turning other authors against her.'"

"Worth the middle-of-the-night call, right?"

"Yes. God. Okay, I have to go. I have to do some damage control. And come to think of it, maybe I should ask Driftwood to put up a preorder link. This is terrible, but all attention is good attention, right?"

"Hey, any way to sell books is a good way."

I opened my email to brief the team and realized I was the last to know. I found six interview requests, twenty-seven angry messages from other writers, and forty-two emails of solidarity. Not a bad ratio actually. But wow—this was insane. If my email was blowing up like this, what were the Fantasticreads folks saying? And it was still dark in LA!

I started texting Michael. But what to say? I decided just to send him the tweet with a sad face emoji. Apparently, my vocabulary bank was empty.

"Mom?"

Zoe appeared in the doorway.

"Hi, love. Oh no! Are you okay?"

She shuffled over to the bed. I could tell she'd been crying, and I stretched out my arm for a hug. Every so often, it felt like she was a little girl again. My book quickly took a backseat. I threw the phone on the bed, accidentally hitting Ethan's leg ("Ow!"), and patted for her to sit next to me.

"What's the matter, love?"

Zoe sniffled. "I think I made a big mistake."

I brushed her hair behind her ear. She never let me do that anymore.

"Okay. Whatever it is, we can handle it. Unless you murdered someone. Did you murder someone?"

She half-laughed. "No."

"Is it Damien?"

"No, Mom."

"Okay, good. So? What is it?"

"I think maybe the tweet you were just talking about on the phone is *my* fault."

"What? How?"

"I told you. I made a big mistake."

"Zoe. Explain, please."

"Some guy called the house yesterday saying he was your new agent. He was joking around and asking me all these questions about

119

how I felt about your book. So I answered and told him more about it since he sounded so official."

My heart skipped a beat. I forced myself to use a more lighthearted tone so Zoe didn't see me completely freak out.

"Okay, now *I* might commit murder. Do you have any idea who he was? Did he leave a name or anything?"

"No, and now I obviously realize he wasn't your new agent . . . and I ruined your new book." Zoe's eyes filled with tears.

"Honey, you didn't ruin my new book. You helped me get my first big hit! Don't even worry. But I *am* concerned that someone cared enough to bother *my daughter* about this. I mean, that is beyond low. Low, low, low."

"So you're not mad?"

She looked at me the way she used to, her eyes wide and vulnerable.

"No, love. I'm not mad at you. In fact, I'm *so* glad that you trusted me enough to tell me the truth. And *while* we're truth-telling, what's up with you and Damien?"

"Nice try, Mom."

We looked at each other and smiled, a brief interlude in the teenage wars.

"Maybe I could get that double piercing now?"

"Nice try, Zoe."

# Eighteen

Michael: Holy crap.

Me: I know.

Michael: How'd they find out?

Me: Some crazy guy got ahold of my daughter on the phone yesterday and said he was my new agent. She told him everything.

Michael: Your daughter? Are you kidding me? Calling HR, PR, anything that ends in R. These guys are ruthless. Do they not have boundaries?

Me: Awful.

Michael: Let's meet in person to discuss next steps.

Me: Okay.

Michael: I'll set it up. See you soon.

Me: Great.

Michael: Pippa?

Me: Yeah?

Michael: You aren't in this alone.

Me: Thanks, Michael.

Michael: 🖤

*WTF.*

# Nineteen

A heart emoji?"

"Yeah. Look, I'll send you all a screenshot."

"This is insane," Gabriela said.

I'd called an emergency book club meeting. Josie was in hair and makeup, a team of people around her as they paired her cobalt-blue dress with matching eyeshadow. Kelly was in a DanceBody workout studio somewhere—they all looked the same—surrounded by women waiting for class to begin, a seemingly pregnant teacher behind her. Gabriela was in the stables in Greenwich, clad in a riding helmet, jodhpurs, high black boots, and a cute zip top, ready to get on her horse. And I was in my Volvo, my hair pulled back with one of Zoe's discarded headbands. I'd thrown on a jean skirt, an LA Dodgers T-shirt, and flip-flops and managed to drop off the kids at school on time. Zoe had actually hugged me goodbye.

"He's totally hitting on you," Gabriela said, brushing her horse's mane.

"Red. Flag. That's all I can say," Josie added. "Be careful. You're married. He's your single boss. You have way more to lose here than he does. And he's notorious for this type of thing."

"He is?!"

"Has he written again since?" Kelly asked.

"He actually asked me to meet him at the terrace restaurant at the Maybourne."

I bit my lip. Kelly's jaw dropped, Gabriela paused midstroke, and Josie shook her head, brushing off the stylist.

"Hollywood hot spot."

"Romantic."

"Can you bring your agent?" Josie suggested.

"I don't have an agent anymore, remember?"

"Crap."

"Well, don't get too dolled up."

"This is book publishing, not Hollywood," I said, turning into our driveway.

"You literally live in LA," Josie added.

"Okay, fine," I said, parking the car. "I get it. I'll be careful. And it was probably nothing. I'm more worried about the creep who reached out to Zoe."

"Pippa, is this *Blank* book really worth it?" Gabriela asked. "Maybe just scrap the whole thing? Come visit me! We can go on vacation. Casa de Campo! Pull the plug."

I shook my head. "I can't. I'm trying to make a point here. I want to create real change."

"Honestly, what do you hope will happen?" Kelly asked. "What's the best-case scenario?"

"I want people to start reading all different kinds of books, not just the ones on the bestseller list. I want aspiring authors to know that when they toil over a manuscript for years and finally get a book deal, people will find their book. I want to give authors some breathing room so they don't have to be full-time marketing machines."

Silence. No one moved or spoke.

"Am I frozen?"

"You're not frozen," Gabriela replied.

"You actually inspired me! Maybe I *should* write something," Josie said.

"But, Pippa, my books *are* bestsellers," Kelly said, walking out of the studio to escape the glares of the other waiting women. "And so was *Poppies*. Do you not want people to keep reading them? Buying them? I've spent my whole career hoping to make it, and now that I've gotten on the list, you want to take away its meaning. This could tank my career!"

"Not at all," I said. "You put in the work and it paid off. You have a fan base. You earned it! It's the other new authors, those without success, that I want to prop up. The ones who really need it."

"I don't know . . ." Kelly said.

A gorgeous blond man who was *definitely not* Gabriela's husband suddenly popped into view, nuzzling her neck from behind.

"Ummm . . ."

"Gaby!" we all exclaimed.

Gabriela covered her face and grinned. "Forget the readers. I have a story brewing here! Focus on your family. Your writing. Not this pet project. Bye!"

The three of us just looked at each other on FaceTime.

"Well," Josie quipped, "*her* pet project doesn't look too bad."

# Twenty

Driftwood had barely gone live with the *Blank* website before more articles began popping up. A protest group formed its own site, BlockBlank.com. Hundreds of people, including many authors, signed a petition demanding the publisher stop production of *Blank*. Clearly, the idea was hitting a nerve.

If I could just get more likes on my real estate site, I'd feel calmer. I needed that. Craved it. Watching the numbers go up and up there felt like taking a Valium. I'd detoured into Bel Air after drop-off for a treat: a modern new build of epic scale. There was a retractable glass patio wall. And a recent price reduction, too! I raced through the house in ten minutes, popping into closets, cabinets, and shelves, trying to find dirt on its occupants, then jetted out to make my meeting with Michael.

I pulled up to the Maybourne only five minutes late after circling Beverly Hills, passing Spago and La Scala, trying to find the entrance to the hotel. And yes, I had gotten a bit spruced up, putting on a long, flowy dress and a trendy hat, plus mascara. But whatever. It was just lunch, and I needed my book project to succeed.

My boots clicked through the marble lobby as I headed into the stunning courtyard, string lights and ivy overhead, tables dotted around the outskirts like we were in a European square. Before I could check in with the host, I spotted Michael perusing the menu and glancing at his watch. Was I that late? And man, he looked *really* good. Powerful. Handsome.

*Oh no. Stop it, Pippa.*

"So sorry! I had trouble finding the entrance," I said, pulling out the chair beside him and sliding in.

"Not at all. I was early," he said, standing up halfway in a nod to old-fashioned manners. I approved.

"Something to drink for you?" The waitress was next to me before I could finish my hello.

"Um, coffee with oat milk? Thanks."

She nodded and I turned back to Michael. His blue eyes sparkled, enhanced by his white button-down shirt with sleeves casually rolled, freshly combed silver hair, and deep-olive skin. He looked like a Giorgio Armani ad. Or was it Acqua di Giò? I don't know. He looked hot.

"Thanks for meeting me," he said. "I don't usually text my authors, but now I'm getting excited about this book and its potential."

"I'm excited, too—and honestly relieved. You know my agent, LeeLee, wasn't exactly a fan, so now there's no one really in my corner."

He shook his head. "I know LeeLee well. No courage. No vision."

I shook my head. He leaned in closer.

"But you. You have *vision*. The way you were talking in that meeting, wow." He leaned even closer and whispered, *"It got me . . . excited."*

I could feel my chest and face flush instantly. What *exactly* did he mean by that?

"And . . . here's your coffee! Oat milk on the side. Will you be needing a spoon with that?"

"No thanks. All good," I said to the waitress. Maybe he meant it showed him how *exciting* it was to work on a successful book? *But why is he scootching over so close to me?!*

We both sat back as the waitress took her time lining up the cup and saucer, theatrically pouring in the coffee from a silver pitcher, then swirling around the oat milk with a little sugar stick.

"Have you had a chance to take a look at the menu? Have you dined with us here before? I can explain a few things—"

Michael cut her off, his hand raised.

"We're actually going to need a few minutes. We'll let you know when we're ready."

"Alrighty," she said. "Well, just so you know, the scones here are excellent. And the ham and cheese special is also wonderful. I'll give you two a few minutes! Can I refill your water, sir, before I go?"

"I'm all set," Michael said.

She finally walked away.

"Good lord."

"You were saying?" I asked.

He turned on that seductive look again. Steamy, like a leading man in an Annabel Monaghan novel. Could he just flip a switch that easily?

"Pippa," he said, "I . . . *see* you." A sentence never more satisfying: *I see you.*

I leaned forward, staring into his eyes. He saw me . . . how? What was the correct way to reply to that statement: "Thanks? I see you, too!"

Suddenly he leaned back and was all business again.

"So. We're fast-tracking *Blank* for publication, as I told you. Sales and PR are *not* happy. But as long as you're ready to go out and talk about the book the way you did in the conference room, then we're good. You have to perfect your shtick. Why it's the perfect book. Why it's important. All that. And you have the monetary motivation as well—and, of course, we hope you can keep publishing with us."

Yes, how could I forget. This was all about money for him. A lump formed in my throat.

"I mean, it's *not* a shtick," I said. "I meant what I said."

"You know what I mean," he added, reaching his hand out to cover mine. "I didn't mean to offend. Of course, you *meant* it."

We both stared at his hand. *My* hand felt like it was on fire. I could literally feel a stirring in my nether regions as he gently danced his fingertips over my knuckles. My face flushed again; I could feel it turning bright red.

"How 'bout now? You two ready to order?"

He snatched his hand back.

"No!" we both said.

But the moment was over.

Under the table, his knee found mine and slowly started moving back and forth. He smiled knowingly.

Oh my god. This, I was not making up.

No matter how miserable I'd been in my marriage and how deprived I was of physical affection, any kind of attention, I'd *never* thought about cheating. I mean, the occasional fantasy perhaps. But not really doing it. I was a family woman. A mom. Devoted. Loyal. No matter how unpleasant life with Ethan could be, I would be faithful. And it was okay, really. This was just the hand I'd been dealt. I was lucky in other ways—just not in my marriage. But I wasn't going to stray from the bedrock of my life, the father of my children. Maybe Gabriela was comfortable doing that, but not me.

But here was Michael. Powerful Michael who really *saw* me. Who was playing footsie with me as my married life flashed before my eyes. *Would I?*

He was looking into my eyes so intensely that I had to look down at my napkin, my body on fire in places that I didn't think could even catch fire anymore. I mean . . .

"So, tell me you're ready to market the heck out of this book," he said.

"Yes," I whispered, nodding too quickly. *Yes, yes, YES,* I thought.

He knocked the table with his fist.

"Good," he said. "*Blank* is the buzz book we've been looking for. I know we both have interest in making it a success. I've pushed a beach read, two historical novels, a thriller, and two memoirs to make room for it. Let's make it huge."

"Wait, what? No, no, please don't do that. Don't push any pub dates. Those authors were counting on their books coming out. They'll hate me!"

This was not good.

"Don't you worry. I'll manage the other authors. This is business. They'll understand. Pippa, I'm ready for *us* to make some book magic together. And besides, you're under contract, remember?"

Did I find his threats . . . arousing?!

He stopped and smiled. I could feel the flush spreading across my chest again. Mental note: *Buy turtlenecks.*

"Now leave the rest to me," he said, rubbing my knee with his thumb.

"Okay, it's that . . . to me, this isn't just business. Did you ever see the old movie *You've Got Mail*, with Meg Ryan and Tom Hanks?"

"No, I don't really watch rom-coms."

"Well, it's more than a rom-com. It's actually a really interesting commentary on the role of business, particularly the book business, and how it affects individuals, like Meg Ryan, who played an indie bookseller."

"Okay. Why are we talking about this again?"

"You said moving pub dates was just business. But in the movie, there's this great scene where Meg says something like, 'When businesspeople say something isn't personal, it means it isn't personal to *them*.' It is personal to many people on the other side of decisions like that."

"Well, she wasn't running a big corporation, was she?" Michael chuckled. My attraction to him quickly dissipated.

"This is my favorite movie line of all time. She goes, 'Whatever else anything is, it ought to begin by being personal.'"

Michael raised a well-groomed eyebrow. "This from an author who's writing a book with no words?"

"But that's a commentary on the industry, on art and creativity!"

"But is it personal? Wouldn't it be a bit more personal if you had, say, a character or two in your book?"

Maybe he had a point. Were we having our first fight?

"I'm trying to defend other authors," I said.

"You do the blank book. I'll run the business. We're pushing other pub dates for yours. You should be grateful." He leaned in close to me and didn't break his gaze. *"Excited."*

"I am . . . grateful, I mean. I really am!"

From nowhere, ponytail #1 and ponytail #2 appeared, flanking him in almost identical black dresses. Ponytail #2 gave the update.

"Michael, there's an emergency with *The Santa Monica Warrior Princess*. You have to get on the phone with Barnes & Noble."

He sighed and reached into his back pocket, pulling out a small envelope.

"A little something," he said, smiling and knocking the table again. "To kick things off right."

I caught the ponytail girls glancing at each other.

I took the envelope and stood up to say goodbye. He reached over and shook my hand, gently rubbing his index finger in suggestive circles on my palm. I bit my lower lip and he let go.

"To be continued," he said. The words were like little pheromone darts, pinging me in all the right places despite my aversion to his business tactics. *Damn it, brain!*

I sank back into my seat and watched him go, my knees now shaking, his touch imprinted on me like an X-ray. He turned back just once and smiled, and then, I swear to god, the man actually winked.

I just sat there with my untouched cup of coffee, staring after him.

"Not staying for lunch, I see?" the waitress said cheerily.

I took a deep breath. "Just a check, please."

"The gentleman already took care of it," she said. "Well, I do hope you'll come back and try our award-winning cuisine. I just had the French toast this morning and, oh my, what a perk." Then she lifted my mug and added, snidely, "Course, looks like *your* job comes with many perks."

"*My* job? No, no, you don't understand . . ."

She held a finger to her lips, as if to say that she'd keep my secret. *But there's nothing to tell!*

"He's a repeat customer," she said, walking away.

I opened the envelope.

It was a key card. Room 767.

*Oh no.*

My phone dinged.

Tonight at 9 pm. See you there.

*Gah! Now what?!*

# Twenty-One

My Volvo screeched out of the hotel driveway, covering the valet outpost in dust. My life felt like it had been blown to bits, too many to pick up. I needed this book to succeed, and for that to happen, I needed Michael. But what to do about the contents of that envelope? I could barely look at it.

I called Gabriela on speaker and shut the windows so no one could hear.

"Is this my favorite author?"

"Gaby, oh my god, the smoking-hot CEO of my publishing company just *hit* on me."

"Aunt Pippa! You're on speaker with the boys."

*Crap.* "Hi, boys! Love you guys! Gaby, can you please take me off speaker?"

"We're driving to practices all over town," she said. "Call you later? But sounds like the plot is *thickening*?" She laughed as I groaned and hung up. I tried Josie next, weaving through the palm trees up Canon Drive.

"You've reached Josie Gray. Please leave me a message."

*Damn it!* "Emergency, call me back!"

Next, Kelly. Kelly *had* to answer. She was always near her phone.

"Kel?" She'd picked up, but I heard rustling noises. "Everything okay?"

"Just leaving yoga," she said, out of breath.

"I thought you were just at DanceBody."

"I was. Big workout day. How'd it go with your publisher?"

"Michael just *propositioned* me. He wants me to meet him tonight *at a hotel*. He gave me a key card like we were in some porno. But honestly, he is so hot and my body is on fire and I've never cheated but I've also never really had the opportunity. Oh my god. What do I do?"

"Pippa, have you ever actually watched porn?"

"What?! Well, no, not exactly, but . . ."

"I mean, I haven't seen anyone give each other key cards. Like, 'Oh yeah, give it to me . . . give me that . . . key card.'" She laughed.

"KELLY! Stop."

She couldn't stop laughing. I thought I heard someone else laughing next to her.

"Who are you with?"

"No one, no one. Okay, okay," she said. "Are you going to do it?"

"Noooo. I don't want to! But I also don't want to jeopardize my book launch."

"The launch of your pretend book?"

"Kelly, come on. Are you on my side or not?"

"I am! It's just this kind of thing happens *all the time*. You're acting like you're the first person. Like the #MeToo movement wasn't a thing."

"Well, it hasn't happened to me," I said quietly. My eyes were welling up with tears. I started imagining what might happen if I went through with it. What if my kids found out? In my haze of infatuation before we got married, I'd been fooled by Ethan. What we had wasn't a happy, fulfilling marriage. I'd had enough relationships to at least know what I wanted in one—and this wasn't it. What now? Should I take the opportunity in front of me? But no. Just because I didn't have the relationship I wanted didn't mean I had to overlook my values.

"Maybe you should go? Have some fun?" Kelly said. "You wouldn't be the first to cheat."

"Honestly, I don't even think I could pull it off. I'm such a bad liar. Wait, have *you* cheated?"

"I plead the fifth."

"*Whaaat?* You have? And you never told me?! Who?"

"Doesn't matter."

"With someone from the publishing world?"

"Well, no."

"Okay," I said, "we're going to have to discuss this in extreme detail."

"Nothing to discuss," Kelly replied. "But look. He isn't your boss. He's your publisher. It isn't exactly a workplace violation. I mean, I guess you could report him—tell your editor. Try to get his ass fired."

"His ass . . ." I sighed, thinking about it.

"Pippa!"

"Sorry! I've just never felt like this."

"Aroused?"

"Funny."

"If this is really upsetting you, then write an editorial. Call him out. Women have been treated like this for far too long."

"But, Kelly, he was actually treating me nicely. He seemed into me."

"It's playing into the patriarchal assumption that—"

"Please," I said, "no more. If I have to hear the word 'patriarchy' one more time, I'll scream. Let me figure this out."

"Blow it out of the water, Pippa. Think about how well *Blank* will do if you bring this scandal to light."

"I mean, I won't *have* a book if I bring this scandal to light."

I paused at the eight-way intersection. How did anyone know when to go? I waited until the Bentley behind me honked. *Ah, my turn!*

"I say report him or actually go through with it and have some fun. Or I can call my contact at *Ellipses* if you want."

"The industry gossip column? No, no, no. Please don't. *Ah*, he has me in the worst position. To earn out my advance, I really need him to get behind the book . . . not behind *me*."

"Who knows what he'll do to you?"

In my head, all I could think was, she didn't know what was being done to me at home.

But no. I wasn't going to the hotel. And I wasn't going to report him. I just needed to make it all go away.

I pulled the car over next to a giant home in The Flats of Beverly Hills.

My hands were shaking as I texted Michael back.

I can't, sorry!

Short and sweet. Three dots flickered back and then, a thumbs-up sign. The head of a publishing house couldn't write a single word.

# Twenty-Two

I headed straight to a four-bedroom on Mandeville Canyon that I really wanted to profile on Instagram. It looked ominous from the listing—a teardown. But maybe it had good bones? *Whatever.* I needed a release, to escape from myself and clear my head. The exterior appeared dark and leafy as I turned left from the road and pulled up in front of the gate. The home was definitely a little sketchy looking from the outside. When I parked, the tail of my car jutted out into the street. No driveway? Not good.

Before getting out, I put on my house-hunting disguise du jour: a blonde wig, extra-large sunglasses, a fedora and scarf, and a Hermès knockoff. Still shaken from my meeting with Michael, I buzzed and the creaky gate opened like a haunted house greeting me. Maybe this one *wasn't* a good idea. But it was represented by The Agency, one of the best brokers in town. I'd just dash in real quick.

"Hello, welcome to Casa Bonita!" A junior agent I'd never seen before offered his hand. He looked like he'd just graduated from Pali High. "Feel free to look around. Here's the floor plan."

"Thank you," I said, trying to disguise my voice. I would not let this doofus blow my cover. "Why are the current owners selling?"

"They bought it intending to renovate but ended up moving out of town. They owned it for many years and just never got things going. The permitting process took longer than they thought it would, and the whole project got too big for them. But thankfully, now the permits are in place so the new owner can break ground immediately."

"Ah, got it."

I walked through the mahogany-paneled dining room into the living room, where the heavy drapes hid all the natural light.

"It would be easy to lighten the place up and make it your own," the agent said, trailing behind me.

I started down the hallway to the bedrooms. When I walked into the master, it was clear to me that the tenants were still living there. Such a distraction. But great for Instagram. I started snapping photos.

"I thought you said the owners moved out?"

"They did, but they're renting it out. They'll be out as soon as it's sold."

The sheets were a bit messy, as if they'd just been slept in. Huge listing faux pas! Clothes—both his and hers—were strewn everywhere in the room and in the walk-in closet. I'd started to walk back out when something caught my eye. The three dresses hanging there in dry-cleaning bags looked just like the ones I'd dropped off a few weeks ago. Hadn't Ethan said he'd pick them up? They were connected by a twist tie to another bag holding blazers and button-downs. Could those be Ethan's? What on earth was our dry cleaning doing in this horrific house?

Ethan usually dealt with the dry cleaning. He insisted on using a company in West Hollywood that he said tailored his clothes to perfection—but they didn't pick up or deliver on the Westside. I walked farther in to get a closer look. Could those really be ours, or was I just losing my mind? Did someone *steal our dry cleaning*? Who would do something like that?

I didn't recognize the other clothes—a few other skirts and tops, plus the two pairs of shoes, which were smaller than mine. My feet were a size 8.5 and these were tiny, like a 6. Although they did look somewhat familiar. Size 2 jeans from Barney's (RIP)? *I wish.* Then I turned to "his" side of the closet. And there, right on top of the hamper, were Ethan's trademark blue pajamas.

*What?!*

I just stared.

I took a few more steps and looked closely. *Lots* of men surely wore those pajamas. But then I recognized a couple of Ethan's T-shirts on the shelves. His favorite sneakers. A pair of jeans I hadn't seen in a while. And on the counter was a bottle of his Lacoste cologne.

WTF, was Ethan *living* here? In this dark, spooky, run-down home? And whose women's clothes were *those*? Why was my dry cleaning here? WHAT WAS GOING ON?

"Um, excuse me?" I called out to the broker. "Are the renters here long term? How many months have they been renting?" I could hear his wing-tip shoes against the dark floors as he made his way into the bedroom.

"Oh heavens," he said, walking into the room. "An unmade bed? I'm so sorry. I forgot to double-check the master—I mean, *primary*—bedroom this morning. The tenants have been here, oh, maybe six months? They go month to month. I promise they won't be an issue. Nice couple. I *told* the owners that renting it out was a bad idea, but they insisted."

"Nice couple? Famous? You can tell me," I said, turning on my charm. "Maybe I know them."

"Oh, I doubt it. They said they just moved here. Barely have any stuff. Know no one. The wife is a doll. One of those workout types. Really light blonde hair. And the husband said he was from . . . oh, where did he say? Somewhere on the East Coast. But they've been overseas for years for his job. Something in finance. They both travel a lot."

*No, no, no.*

It couldn't be.

"Is that right? And why did they say they were here?"

"His job relocated," the broker said.

My husband's clothes.

My dry cleaning.

Kelly telling me she'd cheated on Arthur. Ethan's frequent meetings with actors and plays he had to see. Was he really just fifteen minutes away in Brentwood? With my best friend?

*Oh my god.*

Had they made a little love nest for themselves? Had Ethan been gradually moving over all the clothes he sent to the dry cleaner so I wouldn't notice—and then accidentally brought my dresses, too?

Would Kelly do that to me? Would Ethan?

I watched the broker make the bed and close the closet doors, shaking his head and clucking his disapproval.

"The tenants are supposed to leave it perfectly clean. So sorry, I guess they're in town after all."

I wanted to collapse dramatically into the broker's arms. I felt like I was living in some terrible movie. But it wasn't a movie—it was my life. And I was going to have to walk myself out of the house and back into my car and go about my day like everything I held sacred hadn't just blown up in my face. I could do it. I would do it. I had to. One step. Then another.

I would obviously *not* be posting about this listing.

Or would I?

# Twenty-Three

My hands shook as I drove down Sunset. It was almost time to pick up Max from school. Could my best friend really be sleeping with my husband? And why on earth did they rent a random home in Brentwood? Was something wrong with the eight million hotels in LA?

*Maybe it wasn't an affair. Maybe the two of them were meeting up to plan a surprise party for me! Maybe they—*

No. There was no other explanation.

They were clearly together.

The question was: For how long? The realtor said they'd been renting for six months . . .

*How could they both have betrayed me like this?* Kelly's middle-of-the-night call. Had she been right here, staying at this house? Maybe her whole book tour was a hoax. What about her kids and Arthur in New York? How often had she been out here in LA without my even knowing it?

I pulled into the pickup line at Max's school. Damn it. I would definitely be late getting Max to Hebrew school today, just like I'd been late getting him to chess yesterday. Now I was a failure as a mom, too. As I waited, I checked out Kelly's Instagram. Were there any clues in her photos of book events, casual family shots, and the endless press she was getting for her latest release? The whole best-friend-sleeping-with-husband thing hadn't exactly crossed my mind.

And now she wanted *me* to cause a #MeToo stir about Michael? Probably just to throw me off her scent. What was happening? Had Kelly put Michael up to this? Did they know each other?

My mind kept circling the alternatives, trying to make sense of everything. It felt like *Wheel of Fortune*, the arrow not quite clicking in for the "Win That Vacation" slice, instead landing just a few notches down, at "Bankrupt."

I didn't want to call Josie or Gabriela. What if they already knew? What if everyone knew but me? Who could I possibly trust?

There was only one person I could call.

I envisioned a Palm Springs poolside. An empty glass on the table. The cellphone ringing until a wrinkled, bedazzled hand picked it up.

"Darling!"

"Hi, Mom."

# Twenty-Four

It's hard to be close to an alcoholic. There was always something more important than me. My mom's next drink and her coterie of partiers took the place of milk and cookies, questions about my homework. I envisioned her as warm, loving, and attentive before my dad died. But she was only thirty years old when he died—and when she lost herself, too.

I never blamed her. She'd experienced a lot of trauma. My mom had grown up on the Upper East Side in the lap of luxury, a penthouse on Fifth Avenue. But on her eighth birthday, she was on a carriage ride with my grandmother in Central Park when the horse got spooked by a biker. The horse reared, my mom and grandmother were thrown out, and the carriage toppled onto my grandmother, missing my mother by a fraction of an inch. She lay on the ground next to her mom, unable to help, feeling like it was all her fault. After all, she'd begged for a horse-and-carriage ride, something her mom said "only tourists" did. But it was her birthday wish.

My grandfather, a stockbroker, tried his best to raise Mom and her three sisters, but he suffered his own tragedy. His investments were gutted when he shorted the wrong stock for a client during a market downturn. He didn't just lose all his family's money; he took down his entire firm. Unable to live with what he'd done and seeing no way out, he climbed onto the sixteenth-floor balcony of his workplace and jumped.

My mother started drinking then, in her teens, but nothing dulled the ache enough. The trauma was etched into her very being. To cope, she turned inward, thinking only of herself—unable, really, to feel the emotions of others. It was all too raw. Then her husband, my dad, passed away early. I understood the instinct to dull herself. To put on an act, her Mommy Dearest charade. To take up with a man who lived to flatter her.

I essentially raised myself. When I thought about it that way, it made sense that I was okay with my marriage. I was used to going at it solo, lacking attention and love. Yes, my mother was around when I was growing up, but she was utterly inaccessible. Just like Ethan. I hadn't been able to break the cycle. That's why I was determined that Max and Zoe would feel my love every minute of every day. That they would know what it felt like to be important to someone else.

I rarely turned to my mom for anything.

But I'd hit rock bottom. If my best friend and my husband had betrayed me, who did I really have left?

"How are those beautiful grandchildren of mine?" she cooed.

"They're great, Mom," I said, fighting back tears. "I'm actually in the pickup line waiting for Max."

"All these pickup lines. I still don't know why your kids can't take the bus like everyone else in America. You certainly did."

"I know, Mom. That's just the way we do it here. I live so close to the school, it's really no problem. And honestly, I just can't take any criticism right now."

As my car inched closer to the front of the line, I started crying. Everything was starting to feel real.

"Pippa? What is it? Fine, don't have them take the bus. I was just pointing out—"

"Mom, I think Ethan is having an affair. With Kelly."

Silence. Then: "Well, it wouldn't surprise me. He's never been a nice person, although this is pretty low even for him. But why on *earth* would he do a stupid thing like that? He could have any floozy he wanted!" She laughed a little.

"I don't know. It's not like we've had *such* a happy marriage. But we've been together almost two decades. Our family is my whole life. How could he do this? I mean, I've been tempted—even now I am, by someone—but I haven't *done* anything."

"Darling, no marriage is that happy after almost two decades. But how can you be sure he's cheating?"

"I found all their clothes together in a rental home."

"What? What were *you* doing in someone else's rental home?"

"That's not what's important here. I found his discarded pajamas in the closet next to Kelly's clothes, right here in LA."

"Well, couldn't they . . . okay, well, actually, there is no reasonable explanation. But it doesn't mean they're having an affair."

Someone knocked on the passenger window.

"Mrs. Jones?"

I could see Max and his teacher through the window. I'd forgotten to inch up to the correct pickup spot. I motioned for them to open the door so Max could climb in.

"Hi, Mom," he said, tossing his backpack on the floor and climbing in the front seat. It was so nice to be out of the car seat phase.

"Is that my grandson?"

"Gee-Gee is on speaker," I explained.

"Yeah, I got that," he said, buckling up. "Hi, Gee-Gee!"

"Hi, Max! When are you coming to the desert to visit your old grandmother?"

"You're not old, Geeg!"

"Ah, that's why you're my favorite. Call me any time. And come visit. I'll pay you."

"What's the going rate of a grandmother visit?"

"Kidding, dear. And, Pippa, call me later if you want to keep chatting about that son of a bitch."

"*Mom!!*"

"Sorry, sorry."

I pressed End on the giant dashboard.

"Who's the son of a bitch?"

"Max! No one. Just a guy I'm working with on my book. But tell me about school. Tell me something you learned today that I might not know."

"Um, well, okay. Did you know that Ponce de León was an explorer who was trying to find the Fountain of Youth?"

"Yes, I actually *did* know that. He was just a little ahead of his time. Apparently it's called Botox."

Max chuckled and pulled out a granola bar.

"Do I really have to go to Hebrew school?" he asked. "Why do I need a bar mitzvah anyway?"

"It's how you become a man in the Jewish faith. It's a rite of passage. A tradition, a ritual. It's what boys your age have done since the ancient days. And now it's your turn. Plus, you'll get lots of gifts. Maybe even money. Cash. More cash than you'd get from visiting your grandmother."

He crossed his arms and looked out the window, not saying anything.

"But a bar mitzvah isn't just about the gifts or money; it's about the connection to spirituality. To faith. And community. It's about commitment."

"Good sell, Mom."

"Thanks," I said. "Almost forgot that part."

We both smirked.

"Can I have a service without any guests? Just family?" Max asked. "I don't want to sing in front of my friends."

"If that's what you want, then sure. But why don't we see how you feel after practicing?"

"How many times do I have to go to Hebrew school this year?"

"Oh, about twenty."

"Twenty?!"

"Is that a lot or a little? Let's just start with today. You're going *today*. And I bet you'll meet some nice people."

"Maybe," he said, staring out the window. "You know, Mom, I was kidding about that blank book idea when I first mentioned it, right?"

"I know. But I love it! You're a genius."

He shook his head.

"Mom, I love reading what you *actually* write. Maybe you could come up with something else? Even just a little something? Those essays you write about Zoe and me are so funny, even if you do change our names. The blank book doesn't have you or your funniness or any of that. It's like a total waste. And everyone's mad at you for doing it. It's all my fault. And I didn't even mean it."

I pulled up to a stop sign, put my sunglasses on top of my head, and looked at him closely. He had tears in his eyes.

"Honey. That is the sweetest thing you've ever said to me. I'm so happy you like the way I write. And it is *not* your fault. I'm a grown-up. This was my decision. And I still think it's the right one."

He looked back at me with a hint of a smile.

"I'll still write in my own voice," I said, "I promise. *Blank* is more of a think piece."

"A think piece. Okay."

"What should my next book be about?"

"Me?"

We laughed.

I reached over and grabbed his hand as we drove along in silence. Max periodically Snapchatted pictures of himself and the dashboard.

"Are you and Dad getting divorced?"

My foot involuntarily slammed on the brakes, causing the car behind us to lay on the horn.

"Whoa, Mom! Don't get us killed, okay?"

"Sorry, sorry, sorry. Did *not* mean to do that." I raised one hand feebly to apologize as the tricked-out SUV roared past. "Max, why would you ask me that? We have no plans to get divorced."

"I don't know," Max said. He shrugged and kept looking down at his phone. "I just feel like you guys don't even talk. And Jared's parents just got divorced."

"No way! I always thought Jared's parents were so happy together. Huh. See, you never really know what goes on in other people's homes."

*But how should I respond to his actual question?* No one told me that being a mom required constant psychological intervention.

"Your dad has a lot on his mind these days," I started. "It's not easy going from a famous child icon to sitting on the sidelines. His career isn't going quite as well as he'd hoped, and I think that makes him not his best self sometimes, you know? Plus, my own career took off with *Poppies*. I think that was a little tough for your dad. Even though now I'm back to square one."

"You mean the whole 'I'm a theater producer' gig?"

"Mm-hmm. I mean, he doesn't even *like* the theater."

We chuckled. But I did want to impart some motherly wisdom.

"It's hard for someone's self-esteem to take a hit like that," I said. "We all have flaws, as you know."

How could I defend Ethan when I suspected he was shacking up with my BFF? No matter what, I wanted the kids to have a good impression of their dad. I kept going.

"I think sometimes the issue is that your dad gets a little annoyed with *me*."

"Yeah, maybe you're right."

"I'd do anything to get your dad's attention sometimes. Even write *Blank*."

As I said it, I realized it was true. I would look over in bed at night—not that I'd *ever* tell Max this—and marvel at just how *sexy* Ethan was. When we got together, he had ripped abs, perfect facial features. I mean, he was *hot*. But what happened when you married the hot guy and then he aged and lost all his confidence and joy? My feelings hadn't changed; it was his feelings about himself that were ruining things.

Maybe my ability to run a household, be a present mom, and have my own writing career wasn't exactly a turn-on for *him*. All that stress. All that barking at everyone. Maybe what he wanted was a pretty young thing who made him feel amazing, not a wife who yelled at him for being late to the school play. Although Kelly wasn't any younger than me, they could escape their lives together. Look how easily Michael had tempted me just this morning. What if Kelly had done that to Ethan? But who initiated it? And which was the bigger betrayal?

"Max, did your dad say anything that would make you think otherwise?"

"Nope."

"Okay."

"Never mind," he said. "Shouldn't have brought it up."

"Hey, you can talk to me about *anything*. You know that, right?"

We pulled up to the temple and I put the car in park, turning to hug him.

"Okay, have fun. Meet some new kids. Make someone smile."

He rolled his eyes.

"I'll try," he said, opening the door and grabbing his tattered backpack. "You going to pay me for this?"

"*Pay* you? Not in your wildest dreams."

A few kids ambled into the temple as Max waved goodbye. I held up my hand and signed, "I love you," all but my third and fourth fingers aloft. He made the sign behind his back so no one would see. But I did.

# Twenty-Five

He did *what*?!" Gabriela said.

Gabriela and Josie had finally FaceTimed me back from my hotel-lunch panic with Michael. I was sipping on an iced coffee at a Coffee Bean near the synagogue. Obviously I wasn't dialing in Kelly—and I couldn't admit to the others what I'd just learned. And maybe I was wrong? I couldn't tell the girls until I knew for sure. One hundred percent. So first: Michael's proposition.

"I know, I know," I said. "But, I mean, I . . . kind of . . . liked it. I liked the attention."

"You may have *liked* it," Gabriela said, "but he shouldn't have *done* it! He's your publisher!"

"I know. But *you* do this stuff all the time, Gaby!"

"Ah, but I do it on my own terms. My choice, my rules. It's much better."

"Remember when I profiled Driftwood on my show last year?" Josie asked, wrapping the sides of her knee-length sweater closer in.

I put my cup down on the wooden table. "Yeah? You met him?"

"Oh, I met him alright. And I hate to tell you this, but I've got something I need to show you." Josie started walking around her apartment, then held up something for us to see. I heard Gabriela gasp.

"The same key card?"

"I can't believe it," I said.

"He actually said the SAME THING to me," Josie added. "That he *saw me*. Except after he said it, he put his hand up my skirt, and asked me—"

"Stop," I said. "I don't even want to know."

Josie shrugged.

"You didn't go to the hotel room, right?" I asked.

There was a long pause. Too long. Really too long.

"I went."

"No!"

"You didn't!"

"JOSIE!"

"Oh my god, why didn't you tell us?! What happened?"

"Well, no surprise, he was pretty amazing in bed. And then I never heard from him again."

"Josie!!!"

"I was in and out of the hotel in, like, an hour. Technically he was in and out, if you know what I mean."

I just shook my head as Gabriela said, "Oh, stop with the jokes. You're killing me!"

Josie laughed. "I still get early copies of all the Driftwood books, though, and boy, do I make sure to cover them all on air."

"No!"

"Why?" I asked. "You don't have to do that."

"Well, I didn't want anyone at the studio to find out. I'd be in trouble, too, you know—sleeping with a guest. The talent. Well, not exactly sleeping . . . But he's single and I'm single; we should be allowed to have sex without notifying the company."

"Please stop," I begged, my hand on my forehead.

"Did you fall for it when he said he *saw* you?" Josie asked me.

"He saw me *blush*. That's about it."

Josie and Gabriela laughed.

"And, girl, he's *seen* just about everyone I know," Josie said. "I'm glad you didn't take the bait."

"Why didn't you tell me?" I asked her.

"*Poppies* had come out already. You already had the book deal. I didn't want to mess anything up."

"You know, for all his flaws and all our typical marriage issues, I do love Ethan."

"Of course you do," Josie said.

"We all *love* our husbands, no? It's not only *about* love."

"Gaby, then what's it about?"

"Ah, I think there are many ways for people to love other people. I love Juan Carlos. We have a wonderful partnership. We raise kids together. I help him; he helps me. Attraction? Not anymore. But that's okay. Can one person make another happy in every single way? No. It's too much to ask. So. We decided: We keep our partnership, the ways we love each other, but physically? Not so much. He's not attracted to this version of me, but this is who I am now, and I'm okay with that."

I took a deep breath. "Wow, Gaby. That's really beautiful, actually," I said.

Silence.

"So, wait, does this mean I *shouldn't* publish my book with Driftwood? Should I back out of the deal?"

"Back out of a publishing deal?" Josie said. "Have you lost your mind? Don't you know how hard those are to come by? And why—because he likes to sleep around? Publish the damn book. Michael doesn't *own* Driftwood. He just runs it, and hopefully not for long. But I'd say no more private meetings. And I'd hold on to that key card. Wonder who else is a member of the Michael Key Card Club . . ."

"And how many people *used* their special keys . . . and how *their* books did . . ." Gabriela added.

Just then my phone dinged.

"Hold on, ladies."

Text from Max: Some weird reporter guy just snuck in the classroom. He wants to ask me about Blank. What should I do?

"WHAT?!!?" I said out loud.

I quickly texted Max back: WHAT?!!?

Going into lockdown.

"Holy shit!" I exclaimed.

"Pippa? You okay?" Josie asked.

"No, not okay! Max's Hebrew school is in lockdown, and a reporter snuck in to ask him about *Blank*. Not sure if they're related, but I'm racing over there."

I hung up, grabbed my stuff, and hurried through the crowded coffee shop and back to my car. Soon I was speeding down Montana Avenue.

Max! Are you okay?! On my way.

Under my desk. Just a drill. I think?

You think?

# Twenty-Six

I screeched around a corner, phone in my lap.
Keep texting me, Max. I'm on my way. You okay?

Was the lockdown caused by *Blank*?! Who was this guy sneaking in, and why? I felt like I was going to vomit. But then again, wasn't it naive to think our synagogue would be exempt from the escalating attacks around the world?

I'm okay, Mom.

My phone rang and I looked down to see who it was. *Do I recognize that 424 number?* Stupid Bluetooth wouldn't pair my phone with my car, so I had to swipe to answer. Before I could finish saying hello, I felt a giant WHACK. I'd crashed into the car ahead of me—right in front of that adorable new bookstore I'd been meaning to visit at Eleventh and Montana.

*"Ahhhhh!"*

"Mrs. Jones? Are you okay? Hello?"

Smoke was billowing out from my car's hood. I could see the other driver—a tall, angry-looking man in a leather jacket—getting out of his Maserati.

"Oh no. Oh no. Oh no."

"Mrs. Jones? This is Joshua Lowenstein, Max's Hebrew school teacher."

Now, of course, Bluetooth decided to work and blasted the call on speaker throughout my smashed car.

"I'm sorry. I just got in an accident. I'm trying to get to Max. Is he okay? Are you still in lockdown? Max texted me that there was a reporter there?"

Black Jacket Guy knocked on my window, glaring and motioning for me to lower it. I gave him the "one second" gesture. I appeared to be talking to myself, of course. My phone had flown somewhere into the car's bowels.

"Max is fine. Don't worry. The reporter who came in is also a congregant here, so we didn't think anything of it until he came into my classroom and asked to talk to Max."

"Came into the *classroom*? Was there no security at all? There are antisemitic attacks going on all over the world, and some schmo can just march into the synagogue and into my son's classroom?!"

Black Jacket knocked again. I could hear police sirens.

"I have to go. I was in an accident . . . But Max is okay? No more lockdown?"

"I was caught off guard myself. But I want you to know I followed all the protocols and pressed the buzzer under my desk. Unfortunately, that meant the entire synagogue went into lockdown mode and all students and teachers had to hide under their desks and in closets. But it was just Nathan Jacobson looking for a quote."

"Nathan who? What? Wait, hold on, I really have to go. The police are coming. Are you sure Max is okay?"

"Max is *completely fine*. Mrs. Jones, why don't I stay on the phone in case you need help?"

"Please stop calling me Mrs. Jones!"

Ugh. This was Max's *teacher*. Why was I snapping at him?

I rolled down my window. "I am so, so sorry," I said to Black Jacket Guy. "This was totally my fault. My son's school went into lockdown and I was rushing to get him. He's fine now, but I was racing and I didn't see you and—" I burst into tears. Heaving, sobbing, full-body tears. Kelly. Ethan. Max. Michael. It was all too much.

He held up his hands, disarmed. "Whoa, whoa, whoa. It's okay. Let's just check out the damage here. And is that blood on your forehead?"

I touched my face and felt the stickiness of an open wound.

"Don't worry about me. I just have to get to my son."

Black Jacket Guy and I walked to the back of his car, and he pointed out the smashed taillight and bumper. It wasn't horrific, but . . .

"You got me pretty good," he said.

I couldn't argue with that.

We stood in the middle of the street, looking at his bumper and my steaming car, as the sound of police sirens got louder and a crowd of people formed behind us.

"I'm so sorry. Can I just give you my credit card or something? I really have to get to my son."

"Sure. The police can just grab your information. I have a great bodywork guy. He'll be able to fix this up. Let's just exchange information for insurance."

"Okay, okay, right. I'll grab the forms."

I opened the glove compartment through my passenger-side window and heard, "Mrs. Jones? I'm still here. Everything okay?"

"Oh my gosh. You can hang up!"

"I'll stay on until you get on your way. Max is concerned."

"Wait, put Max on."

My butt was sticking out of the car when I heard the police officers approach. Instinctively I covered my ass and turned around quickly.

"License and registration please, ma'am."

"Hi, Mom!"

"Hi, Max! I'll be right there. Just got in a little fender bender. You okay?"

"Yep. Got some great snaps."

I smiled. "I'm dealing with the police. Be there soon."

"Okay, Mom. I'm totally okay. Hope you are, too."

I handed over the information and got another look at Black Jacket Guy. He looked a little familiar, but then again, most people in LA did.

"Your son okay?" he asked. "I have three kids myself."

"Oh yeah? How old?"

"Six, nine, and twelve."

"Oh nice. Max is twelve and Zoe is fifteen."

We nodded and smiled.

"Where do your kids go to school?" I asked.

"We live over in La Cañada. They go to the public school there."

"Ah. We're in the Palisades."

He nodded. Smiled.

The police handed my information back and took Black Jacket Guy's.

"Holy—it's Derek Johnson!" one cop said to the other.

"No way!"

Black Jacket Guy held up his hands. "Guilty as charged."

I looked from the open-jawed cops to Black Jacket Guy and back again. "Sorry, should I know who you are?"

He laughed. "Nah, you're good. I play for the LA Rams, is all."

Why did people say, "You're good?" I wasn't *good*. But seriously? I hit an NFL player?

Sheepishly, I asked, "What position?"

"Running back."

"Ah."

"Know what that means?"

"Ummm . . ."

He laughed.

"Want to sign my registration? Autograph for my son?"

"Sure," he said, taking it out of my hands. "My number's on there, too. Call if you have any issues with the car."

"You're free to go, ma'am. But we're gonna keep Derek Johnson here for a few more questions."

"Thanks, everyone," I said, walking back over to my car.

I got in, revved the engine, and started to pull back into the traffic, waving to Derek Johnson and the cops as I drove off. Though it was smoking, my car still seemed to be running just fine. Thank God. Maybe God knew I was on my way to the synagogue and needed help.

Then, from the car's speakers: "I'm still here if you need anything." I almost jumped out of my seat.

"Jesus Christ! I almost got in another accident!"

"Not exactly *him*," Josh Lowenstein said.

"I'll be there in a couple minutes. I—" Suddenly, I just couldn't keep it all in. I bit my lip to stem the flow of tears, but the floodgates opened anyway. "I'm trying to get there!" I sobbed. "But do you really want to know what's going on? My entire life is falling apart. My husband, who barely likes me anyway, is apparently in a secret relationship with *my best friend*. My career is *ruined* because I decided to publish a blank book, and now it's become a huge mess and no one will ever take me seriously as an author, plus the publisher wants to sleep with me and I said no, so I'll probably never get another book deal.

"My car is basically on fire right now. I caused my son's whole class to go into LOCKDOWN, as you know. I've apparently *ruined* my daughter's chances of getting into a good college because I couldn't find her an adequate summer program. I don't know who to trust. I haven't had an orgasm since three presidents ago, and—not that anyone will ever notice—my nether regions are going gray. Not even gray. White! WHITE! What am I supposed to do? My. Life. Is. Over."

I was heaving sobs. The leather steering wheel was drenched.

"I mean, really," I cried. "Could things get any worse?"

"Mrs. Jones, I—"

"I am not Mrs. Jones! That's my crazy mother-in-law, Lisa, from Long Island. Call me Pippa, okay?"

Silence.

"Hold on, I'm pulling up right now. I'm so sorry. I shouldn't have said all that . . . Hello?"

# Twenty-Seven

Finally. Max! I could see him in the crowd outside! And he was smiling and talking to a new buddy like nothing had happened. Had I overreacted? I jammed my car, practically sideways, into the first spot I saw (parking skills are overrated), jumped out, and ran over to him.

"Honey! Are you okay?" I threw myself at him, clutching his thin frame in a death grip. I never wanted to let go.

"Mom, relax! It was just one reporter. He wasn't an armed terrorist or anything. He just wanted to ask me about your book."

"My stupid *book* really caused all this?" I pulled back, dismayed, and surveyed the scene of kids, teachers, congregants, police, and parents. Just perfect.

"Yeah, well, I told him *Blank* was awesome."

"So there's that. You're the best. I love you so much," I said, kissing the top of his head and hugging him one more time, shocked he was finally letting me get within five feet of him in public.

"Love you, too, Mom."

"Mrs. Jones?"

I turned to thank his teacher. Who was this Mr. Lowenstein anyway?

"I'm so sorry," I started to say. "I—"

*Wait.* This was Mr. Lowenstein?! This guy didn't look like a Hebrew school teacher. With light-brown wavy hair and a receding hairline, green eyes framed by rimless glasses, and slightly weathered skin, he looked more like a former ski instructor. Pink cheeks. Long eyelashes. A little paunch. A fleece vest over a flannel shirt with the sleeves rolled up. Jeans and sneakers. A friendly smile. He looked like someone who gave great hugs when he wasn't hiking, fishing, skiing, or surfing. But there was something about him that looked really familiar . . .

*No.*

*Hold on.*

"Mrs. Jones?" he said again, softly. "*Pippa* Jones? From Camp Kaleeho?"

"You're that guy!" I covered my face, mortified. "Oh my god, I can't believe I just told you all that about my life."

"*What* guy? You two know each other?" Max asked.

"You're not going to believe this," I said to Max, putting my arm around him. "But Mr. Lowenstein and I went to brother and sister sleepaway camps a hundred years ago. He was the one from the dance who was good friends with Deodorant Guy!"

"Deodorant Guy?" Josh asked.

I turned back to him, pulling my hair behind my ears. "Remember that dance when your friend Fred wore two polo shirts and put deodorant on his face so he wouldn't sweat?"

He nodded, smiling. "I taught him that."

"No!"

"Yep. We all used the same deodorant, by the way. But it worked."

"Unbelievable."

I turned back to Max.

"Mr. Lowenstein and I also starred in the camp play together. I was Wendy and he was Peter Pan." Now looking at Josh, I added, "Remember that scene when we had to ride on the counselor's shoulders?"

"Yeah, and they dropped the guy who played John?"

"Too funny," I said.

A group of students ran over to Josh.

"No more class today, right?"

"No more class," he said. "Just hang out in the courtyard until your parents get here. We called all of them. They should be here soon."

"Yes!" one of the kids said.

"Woo-hoo!" said another, as they raced off.

"Josh, you were, like, the coolest kid in the whole camp. I remember my first day like it was yesterday, and you and that girlfriend of yours—Lauren, was it?—were at the flag-raising ceremony just totally running the place."

"That was before I met *you* and you stole my attention," he said, laughing.

Max gave us both a look.

"Are you in touch with people from camp?" I asked. "I assume you aren't still friends with Lauren?"

"No, actually, Lauren passed away from breast cancer a few years ago, but we were still in touch. And I keep up with some of the others on Facebook."

"Oh no! I'm so sorry to hear that."

"Yeah. I actually went to the funeral. Steve, the camp director, showed up."

"Oh wow, I wish I'd known."

Max scanned the crowd as Josh and I caught up. "Uh, Mom? There are, like, eight million other people waiting to talk to Mr. Lowenstein."

Josh looked down at Max. "I think we should call it a day, buddy."

"Uh, okay. Bye, Mr. Lowenstein."

"Bye, Max. See you next week?"

Max shrugged and looked around at the scene. "Um . . . maybe?"

Josh raised his eyebrows. "Just maybe?!"

"Of *course*," I said, putting my hands on Max's shoulders from behind and leading him toward the car. I looked back at Josh, the temple, the police managing the post-lockdown chaos. The sea of frantic parents. The drama.

"Hey Josh," I yelled, "you don't tutor, do you?"

Zibby Owens

He laughed. "For you? Anything." He pulled his phone out of his vest pocket. "I have your number right here from our call before. I'll text you sometime." His phone case said "I'd Rather Be Skiing." *I knew it!*

"Are you, like, the best Jewish skier in the world or something?" I asked.

He grinned. "Something like that."

Max looked back and forth between us like he was watching a tennis match.

"Should we get home to *Dad*?" he asked.

"Yes, totally."

My phone dinged.

"That was me," Josh said. "Text back so we can find some dates . . . for tutoring."

"Of course. Yes. Dates," I said, blushing.

He walked over to me, telling a few waiting parents that he'd be right with them. "Actually, I could swing by after the rest of the kids get picked up. Half day—hey!"

"Oh, today? Um, sure. Maybe just for a short session so you get all set up for tutoring?"

"That works. Here, type in your address and I'll meet you there after all this hubbub is over?"

He handed me his phone. I mean, how *urgent* was tutoring? The bar mitzvah wasn't for months. But maybe he could tell I was a mess and that I might just need some help tonight. I knew my mascara must be smudged all over my face, my eyes red and swollen like I'd just finished watching *Terms of Endearment*. A pity tutoring session.

Max shook his head. "Oh man! I thought I got out of this whole thing."

"We won't do a whole session, buddy. Just a few prayers today. Then we can start for real next time."

"Are you sure?" I asked. "We can totally wait. Today is insane."

"All good. I'll be right behind you."

166

# Twenty-Eight

N ice parking job, Mom. And nice bumper. Jeez."
"Shut up, Max," I joked, as we got in the front seats. "Not my
best driving day, okay?"

As I headed home, the events of the day slowly sinking in while
Max snapped his friends, I sighed deeply.

"You know, you did the right thing by texting me," I told him.

"I know, Mom. I wasn't as worried as you thought I'd be. But yeah,
lockdown was kinda scary."

"I bet. Max. Can you get off your phone for two seconds? Mini
Mom lecture coming."

"Oh boy. Bet this'll be a good one." He put his phone on his lap,
face up.

"Seriously. I am so, so, so deeply sorry that *anything* in my career
or my life is affecting you or making you feel scared or uncomfortable
or unsafe in any way. None of it is as important as you and Zoe are to
me. Not even close. I would throw all my books away—never work or
write again—if it meant you would be safe and happy forever."

"Aw, thanks, Mom," he said, rolling down the window to let in the
ocean air. "But I want you to be happy, too. I know you love writing
and *Blank* will be great."

But really. Who cared what books I wrote? Who cared about open
houses, Instagram followers, cheating spouses, lecherous bosses. It
didn't matter. All that mattered was keeping my kids safe, happy, and

protected. Doing everything I could to make *their* lives better. Without that, I had nothing of value. Speaking of which, I hoped Zoe was on her way home.

"Can Mr. Lowenstein tutor me instead of me going to Hebrew school? That sucked."

"For a while, yes."

"Good. Because I *really* don't like Hebrew school."

"You went for, like, twenty minutes. How could you possibly know?"

"Oh, I know."

"Honey, there are things in life you have to do, even if you don't love every minute of them. Like Hebrew school. Or learning trigonometry. Or memorizing the elements of the periodic table. But in this case, I'm okay with tutoring. You're completely behind on your bar mitzvah prep. You need to step it up."

"Hey, go easy on me. I was just in lockdown because of you, remember?"

"Good point."

"Just kidding, Mom. It's all good."

He smiled and picked up his phone again.

Now, when was I going to get the car fixed?

———

Zoe, who'd heard about the synagogue lockdown because it was all over Instagram, was waiting for us on the front porch.

"Max! Cutie! Are you okay?" She ran over and hugged him, something I hadn't seen her do in years, basically since she got her first phone.

"Um, what happened to my obnoxious sister?" he joked, hugging her back.

"Shut up," she said, smiling. "This whole thing with you today, Max, has made me reconsider the entire meaning of life."

"Oh yeah?" I said, opening the front door. "It's only been, like, an hour."

"It was enough. I'm over Damien. I'm over Todd. All of them. I'm thinking about living the single life for a while."

"Fabulous," I said. "That's the new meaning of life? Now could you pick up your stuff from the porch and come inside? It's starting to get cold."

———

There was one more thing I had to do.

"Hey, beautiful," Michael said, picking up on the second ring. "Am I seeing you later?"

I hid in my closet with the door closed.

"No. You're not seeing me later," I said. "First of all, I'm married. It's that convention where you stay with someone until death do you part, no matter how miserable you are."

He laughed. "Love that—miserable. Funny! This is why you're a Driftwood author. Did you know that no one's getting married anymore? It's a thing of the past. It went away with Gen Z. They're all like, 'Why would I do that?'"

"I didn't say I was *getting* married. I've been married. For seventeen years."

He whistled. "That's a long time."

"Tell me about it."

"Faithful or unfaithful?"

"Him or me?"

"Both."

"Me, yes. Him . . . not so much, apparently."

"Aha!"

"But here's the thing. This afternoon, a reporter snuck into my son's Hebrew school classroom to ask him about *Blank*. It caused the whole synagogue to go into lockdown. The Hebrew school teacher is literally on his way over here, he feels so bad this whole thing happened. And a reporter called my daughter yesterday and tricked her into telling him about the book. That's what we were *supposed* to talk about at our lunch. This one crazy reporter, Nathan Someone-or-other, harassed both my kids. This has all totally crossed the line and it needs to stop. It's one thing to bother me; I just don't pick up any unknown numbers. Or, actually, known numbers aside from my closest friends and family. Reporters, I avoid. But to harass and threaten my family?"

"That's terrible! I completely agree. What makes you think *I* can stop it?"

"Well, if *you* can't find a way, then I'm going to press harassment charges for your key card stunt, and I'll tell the world that you planted those stories to boost press and sales for the book. And I'll let everyone know about our deal for *Blank*, exactly how many books I need to sell, and the number of your hotel room."

"You wouldn't do that." Pause. "Would you? And man, I *should've* planted those stories! Next time. Good idea!"

"*Not* a good idea. But would I go to the press about you? To protect my kids, I'd do absolutely anything."

"You know I didn't leak any of this, Pippa. Believe it or not, I've got more important things to do than talk to the media about one of the 237 books that we're publishing."

"Do you have 237 room keys?"

"Ouch."

"Well, it doesn't matter if you're the one who leaked it. I just know that you can put an end to it. I heard you got Nobu delivered on a sailboat in the middle of the South Pacific, Michael. You can get anything done! Just please leave my kids out of this. Yes, I want to fight for authors and inspire reading and all of it. But my kids mean everything to me. My son even likes my writing voice, if you can believe it."

"Yes, I can believe it. I'm the one who gave you that two-book deal, remember?"

"You need to help me. Or I can't publish this book."

"Understood. This side of you . . . it's hot," he purred.

Ugh. Michael was the kind of guy who'd have a pussy pad bed, like in that open house. *Wait. That's genius!*

"Michael, I have another idea for how to market *Blank*. And we don't need creepy paparazzi reporters. I have a way to distribute copies to lots of homes. Hold on, the doorbell's ringing. I bet it's the tutor. Man, he got here quickly."

I hung up the phone and ran downstairs. Of course Max and Zoe were both sitting in the kitchen, staring at their phones.

"Guys? Hello? Can't you hear the door? You're, like, *right* next to it!"

No reaction. I shook my head and opened the door.

"Thought maybe I had the wrong house," Josh said.

"I mean, seriously. Look! They're both sitting right here. Max and his sister, Zoe. Did they get up? No."

Josh laughed and walked in. "Teenagers. Totally get it. Welcome to my world." He held up a finger to say he needed a sec. "Hey, Max, did you hear they released some new Pokémon characters?"

"Wait, what?" Max jumped up.

"See? Easy," Josh said. "Teens don't hear doorbells."

I laughed. "I didn't realize it was such a pervasive issue. Perhaps I could get a special doorbell chime that says, 'iPad! iPad!'"

"Not a bad idea," Josh said. Then he turned to Max. "You ready, buddy? Show me what you were working on."

"Okay, I think it's all shoved under the computer," Max said, walking over to it.

"I see—a place of real importance. Maybe we could shove it on top of the computer next time. Really elevate the material."

Max snickered.

"You two good?" I asked.

"All good. We'll get started over here," Josh said, "and stay out of your way."

"And none of the other parents or police or anyone needed you at the temple?" I asked.

"Nope. I spoke to everyone, gave my report, all of it. It was nice to hightail it out of there."

"Hey Mom, what's for dinner tonight?" Max asked.

"Frozen pizza?" I shrugged. "Chicken nuggets?"

"A real chef," Josh joked.

"Hey! It's been a rough day," I said, laughing. "You are *more* than welcome to stay for some chicken nuggets after you meet with Max. If you're lucky, I'll even throw in some pasta. But don't count on it."

"Thanks, I'm okay," Josh said. "I have plans later. But happy to sit and chat while this guy eats."

"Mom, seriously? Chicken nuggets again?" Zoe called from the living room.

"If you'd like to cook, Zoe, then you can come up with the menu," I yelled back. "I've had a long day and don't have the mental energy to *think* of anything to cook."

"Hah! You think *you've* had a long day," Zoe said.

"Okay, that's enough, thank you."

I opened the freezer and pulled out the blue chicken nuggets box.

"Should we go work somewhere else?" Josh asked from the kitchen table while I fumbled around for the right-size pan.

"No, no, it's fine. I'm just going to *cook* here quietly."

As I tore off a piece of tinfoil and sliced some red peppers into strips for dinner—*Take that! I'm cooking!*—I overheard Josh and Max discussing the haftorah portion. Snippets of Hebrew prayers permeated the air. This was my typical podcast-listening time, but tonight I felt like I was in my grandparents' home celebrating the High Holidays or Passover—the language so comforting and familiar, like spotting a photo of a close friend in an unexpected place. Best of all, Josh and Max kept laughing.

By the time I used my college spatula to slide the chicken nuggets and pepper strips onto plates adorned with mozzarella balls and some grapes, I was completely on board with tutoring.

"Well, look what the chef made," Josh said, packing up his materials.

"Not too shabby, right? You sure I can't tempt you? I make a mean smiley face out of ketchup."

He put his hand on his belly. "Tempting, but I have to pass."

"Big plans tonight?"

"Oh, I'm just seeing an old friend," he said.

"Ah."

I wondered who the friend was. Man? Woman? Where were they going? A bar? A restaurant? And why on earth did I care?

"Well, Max, I'll be back tomorrow for the real session," he said. "But I'm glad I could be here after the whole lockdown fiasco."

"Me, too," Max said. "And sorry we caused it."

Josh laughed. "We?"

"Okay, *me*," I said. "Let me walk you out."

Josh fist-bumped Max goodbye and headed to the door in front of me.

"Lovely home you've got here," he said. "Can't wait to come back."

"That's very kind," I said. "Maybe one of these days you'll stay for dinner and I'll actually cook."

"I'd love that," he said. "Looks like you've got more skills than you let on. Hoping your cooking is better than your driving."

"Hey!"

We laughed.

"Alright, good night, Pippa."

I closed the door behind him and let my hand linger on the door handle until I heard his car drive away.

I couldn't wipe the smile off my face.

# Twenty-Nine

The kids were finally asleep. I climbed into bed clad in my green "Do Not Disturb" jammies, pulled the fluffy duvet on top of me, and grabbed my reading glasses. I opened the memoir I was reading: *My What-If Year*. It was about a woman who took on four internships in careers she'd always wanted to try. I couldn't put it down; all I wanted to do was escape my life. *What if . . . I published a blank book? What if . . . I locked my husband out of the house?* Ethan was still out, probably with Kelly, whose texts I'd been ignoring.

How's Max? Heard about lockdown! she'd texted.

Hours later: Pippa? How's Max? Hello?

Then just now: Earth to Pippa. Come in Pippa.

But how was I supposed to respond? She was probably texting me from that creepy house, my husband next to her in his faded blue pajamas. After twenty-five years of friendship, how could she betray me like that?

I didn't have the energy or fortitude to confront her after the day I'd had. Discovering their clothes in the open house. The synagogue lockdown. The car accident. I mean, seriously. I was ashamed, embarrassed, and exhausted.

When my phone dinged, I thought it was Kelly again.

But instead: Hey Pippa. It's Josh, Max's Hebrew school teacher.

I stared at the words.

Hi Josh. I know who you are! You literally just left.

Hahaha, he wrote. Wanted to confirm the time for tomorrow.

Would 5 pm work?

I can make that work.

Great. Stay for Shabbat dinner after! We eat at 6 pm. I promise to actually make something.

So nice of you. Would love to.

Food allergies? I asked.

I'm gluten-free, vegan, have a sesame allergy, and only eat products farmed within 20 miles of where I'm eating. Plus, I'm doing keto right now.

I just stared at the phone. Oh, come *on*. Really? I tilted my head back and closed my eyes. Why was everyone in LA so weird about food?

Kidding! I eat everything. 😋

Oh thank god.

That's what we'll be doing tomorrow. Thanking God. In Hebrew!

See you then. Good night!

Good night, Pippa.

And then, a kissy-face emoji. *Did he mean to send that?* I glanced around my bedroom like someone might be watching.

Oops! Meant that to be a sleepy face! he wrote.

Hahaha. Too bad. 😆

Look forward to meeting your husband tomorrow.

*Point taken.*

He'll probably be at a work dinner. But feel free to bring your wife!

Single. Just me, he said. And my black lab.

Great! Bring the lab. Name?

Dayenu.

Hahahaha.

I'm serious.

Hahahaha, again.

See you two then.

I sent three kissy-face emojis as a joke. Sort of.

# FRIDAY

# Thirty

I had three messages.

One I'd missed from Josh the night before: See you then!

One from Black Jacket Guy, Derek Johnson: Hey. My bodywork guy says he can fix the car for less than insurance wants to pay, so we're good. Let me know if you want some Rams tickets.

Oh, that could be fun. Yes please! I wrote back.

And one from Michael: I called all my media contacts to raise hell. Hoping that puts an end to everything.

Finally! Nothing a little blackmail couldn't fix.

But none from Ethan. And he wasn't in bed.

———

Michael had Brittany send out a press release first thing in the morning, East Coast time. He called out the media's egregious behavior and lack of respect for the privacy of public figures, including authors. He publicly threatened to stop advertising Driftwood books in all newspapers and magazines that depended on their ad revenue for survival. And he vowed to set up surveillance for my kids, me, and even Ethan, plus all Driftwood authors that needed it.

The papers ran the story online within the hour. Then public radio, social media, and even *Ellipses*, the gossip rag, ran a version of the story. I was bombarded by Google Alerts with my name.

BLANK DRAWS THE (INVISIBLE?) LINE
CEO Michael Bostwick lays down the law
Bestselling author Pippa Jones speaks out against the media's invasion of her family's privacy
Desperately Searching Media Sanctions
Don't Make a Pip: Reporters Must Say Mum's the Word
*He really did it!*

I popped online to check my rankings. Preorders for *Blank* had gone *through the roof*—my ranking had gone from #2,435,003 to #6!

"Mom! Chocolate chip pancakes today?" Max yelled from the kitchen.

"Coming!" I said, throwing back the covers. "You'll never believe what happened overnight."

I walked into the kitchen and started making a cup of coffee. Zoe glanced up from scrolling through TikTok videos at an alarming speed.

"Hi, Mom."

"Hi, Zo. Did you sleep well? Still committed to the single life?"

My text dinged with a note from Michael: Turn on DNN.

"Zoe, can you turn on the Digital News Network? You're closest to the remote."

"I'll do it," Max said, grabbing the remote from the TV stand. I stood in the kitchen, gripping my mug with two hands, elbows resting on the island.

And there it was. The whole story. A shot of the synagogue's exterior. My book cover. An artsy image of a phone. A crowd of paparazzi. All the headlines flashing across the screen. Photos of me doing author signings, posing for photos, my author picture.

I felt like I was standing in front of some fun-house mirror, watching myself distort into various shapes and sizes.

"Mom, this is so cool," Zoe said. "You did it! You made a point even before the book came out! You're, like, making a difference. Changing the world!"

"Nice picture," Ethan said, ambling through the back door.

"Dad!"

Zoe and Max hopped up and ran over to give Ethan a hug. Why did he always get the hero's welcome?

"Nice of you to join us," I said.

"I had an all-nighter with that theater crew I told you about," he said, not even looking me in the eye. How had I missed all the signs?

*What a liar.* I just stared at him. Now I knew, but did he know that I knew?

I wished I could go back to pretending that our marriage hadn't completely blown up, that I hadn't been betrayed by the people closest to me. It was hard to process just how hurt, angry, depressed, and foolish I felt.

*What next? Should I leave?* But where would I even go? It's not like I could run over to my mother's (not that I'd want to)—the kids had school in the morning.

Voice from the TV: "Will *Blank* be worth the trouble? Find out this summer when it hits bookshelves."

"Well, you certainly got the press you were hoping for," Ethan said.

"I guess so."

"I hear a certain CEO might be helping with some tempting offers?"

"How on earth would you have heard that?"

"Just some rumors circulating . . ."

"Or did you hear them from a close friend?"

Ethan opened the fridge and grabbed a can of iced coffee.

"Mom, what are you talking about?" Max asked.

"Nothing, love," I responded. "Just joking with your dad."

"Dad, were you really out all night? That's so badass," Zoe said. I just rolled my eyes.

"What can I say? I'm a cool cat."

"Meow?" Max added. I laughed out loud.

Ethan ruffled Max's hair and walked across the kitchen toward the stairs. "I'm heading upstairs for a nap."

"Wait, are you home for Shabbat dinner tonight? Max's new bar mitzvah tutor is joining us."

"Since when is Max getting tutored?" Ethan asked.

"Since yesterday when the synagogue was on lockdown. Did you even want to ask me about that?"

"I spoke to the kids about it yesterday," he said. "It was because of you, right? Max told me everything."

Ouch.

"And how much is tutoring?" he asked.

"Let's discuss when we aren't around the kids."

"Fine. And no, I'm not home tonight. This famous playwright is coming to town and I said I'd join him."

"Oh yeah? What's his name?"

"Oh, you wouldn't know him. He's this very esoteric theater icon. Only those in the industry have heard of him."

"So it isn't . . . say . . . a certain woman?"

*"What are you talking about?"*

"Oh, I don't know."

He gave me a side-eye, but he was doing that thing where he twisted his watch around his wrist. His tell. And then he headed upstairs.

It was all the answer I needed.

"Kids, go grab your stuff," I said. "We're leaving for school in five minutes. Zoe, don't you have some last-minute homework to do?"

"Nope, did it all."

"All of it?" I said, opening the freezer to see what I had for dinner. *I can't serve chicken nuggets on Shabbat.* Then I slammed it shut. Who cared about dinner when my family was falling apart?

"Hey, Mom? I heard Megan Bolero is coming to town!" Zoe said. "Can you get some concert tickets for my friends and I?"

"My friends and *me.*"

"No, not your friends, Mom."

"No, not *my* friends. Never mind. I was correcting your grammar."

"Whatever. Oh, also? I need a black tank top, a pair of leggings, and special dance shoes for our performance on Monday."

"Monday? What are you performing as—the night sky?"

Zoe looked up, unamused. "Funny. No. I'm going to be one of Henry VIII's wives in *Six*."

"Okay, fine," I said. "Do some competitive online shopping. Find what's cheapest and send me the links. Or run over to Target in Westwood with Greta. They might have something."

"Can we get matching outfits?"

"I thought she was canoodling with some guy you liked?"

"Can we not discuss canoodling, please?" Max interjected.

"Mom! Keep everyone straight. No. Greta is amazing. She's like my total BFF. Forever!"

"You don't have to say forever. It's implied in BFF. That's what *best friends forever* means. Best. Friends. Forever. It's like when people say, 'RSVP, please.' RSVP means 'Respond, please' in French. So that's like saying, 'Respond, please, please.' And be careful because you never really know who your best friends are, do you?"

"Whatever, Mom. *You're* acting weird."

"And no, you can't get Greta a tank top. Her parents can get it for her."

"They won't let her wear it. Come on, please?"

I sighed. "Sorry, love. I'm having a tough morning. If you want to say 'BFF forever,' go ahead." I picked up my keys. "Ready for school?"

Zoe looked me up and down. "I'm not trying to put any judgment on this, but I did want to point out that you're wearing your pajamas."

"Ah yes, so I am," I said. "No one will notice; I'm not even getting out of the car."

"Wait," Max said. "If *you* don't have to change, why should we?"

"Because I'm not the one going to school all day. And when I write, I like to wear pajamas."

"I thought you weren't writing anything," Zoe said.

"I just might have an idea," I replied. "Now go get your stuff. We're leaving in two minutes!"

"I'd just like to say that you still have not made me chocolate chip pancakes," Max said, grabbing his backpack. "What's a guy gotta do to get a few pancakes around here?"

"Oh, Max. I completely forgot. I started talking to your dad . . ."

"Aaaaand, now you're making more excuses," Zoe said.

"Just get in the car," I said, affectionately bopping her head.

"Love you, Mom," she said, giving me a little squeeze.

"Love you, too, Zoe. I'm sorry, Max. I promise. Tomorrow. Pancakes. I'll do it!"

But after dropping the kids, I headed straight back to Mandeville. I wasn't laughing anymore. I knew just what bed Ethan was headed to—and it wasn't upstairs in our house.

# Thirty-One

Maybe this was a bad idea.

I steered my battered Volvo past the grazing horses as I drove up the canyon, heading all the way up the hill until I reached the home I'd visited the day before. It felt like a thousand lifetimes had passed since then.

Ethan's car was outside next to what looked like a rental car. Kelly's. My heart pounded in my chest.

What if I confronted them and something terrible happened? What if they were running some *Breaking Bad*–like drug ring?

I slammed my car door shut, steam still pouring out from under the hood. Whatever, I'd get it fixed eventually. I bent down and adjusted the tongue of my sneakers and cuffed my pajama pants, which were pooling around my ankles. Getting dressed was so overrated. Then I checked to make sure the drawstring wasn't hanging down from my waist. I pulled down my top and zipped up my vest, adjusted my ponytail. Took a deep breath. I was ready.

I tiptoed to the window and slowly raised my head to glance into the living room. Empty. Then I crept around the side of the house; that's where the bedroom was. Tiptoe. Tiptoe. The grass was still wet with morning dew. Birds rustled through the thick tree leaves. I felt like I was cut off from the rest of the world. This was not good.

But I had to find out what was happening.

Then I heard it.

I knew those sounds.

The window to the bedroom was cracked, and I cautiously peered inside, knowing but not wanting to process what was happening. But then—

*No.*

*No, no, no.*

*Oh my god.*

There they were. Together. *See? I knew he wouldn't stay in our house sleeping while the kids were in school. He probably only came home to convince himself he was being a good dad.*

Kelly was wearing a white lace bra—and nothing else—and straddling my husband in bed. He was still in his plaid shirt from that morning—unbuttoned—with no pants. Kelly was rocking back and forth as he held her hips and moved her up and down. His bare legs stuck out in front of him, his eyes closed. I watched in horror, like I was witnessing a train wreck.

"Don't stop," he growled. "Keep going."

Kelly's face was turned to the ceiling, her eyes closed, as she held on to his shoulders, going faster and faster, until he called out, "I'm coming! I'm coming!" And then he let out that guttural animal noise I'd heard him make so many times. And, like clockwork, he pushed Kelly off of him and she toppled onto the bed. Some things never changed. But then Kelly got back up and sat on his face, holding on to the headboard as he licked her until she called out, spent. I guess I was the only one willing to sacrifice my needs.

Why was I watching? *What was wrong with me?!* But I couldn't turn away.

They lay on the bed, panting. Ethan was face up, completely exposed, shrunken, his hand lightly gripping Kelly's ass as she rested on her stomach. Maybe it was *me* he didn't want. Maybe *I* didn't turn him on. Maybe I never had. So why did he even marry me?

I sank to the ground beneath the window, my knees curled into my chest, head on my knees, arms wrapped around my head. If I made myself small enough, maybe I could disappear.

I'd never be able to get those images out of my head.

But then some piece of me, a piece I didn't even know existed, clicked into action. Fury. Blind rage. All those years of putting up with Ethan's *bullshit*. Of never being satisfied. Of being ignored, tossed aside. The complete void of affection, the lack of partnership—all of it. It bubbled up in a cloud of venom.

*F them.*

I stood up, raised the window with both hands, and screamed, *"You assholes!"*

"What the—"

"Holy shit," Kelly said.

They both sat up and stared right at me. It felt like a made-for-TV movie. How was this my life?!

*"How could you?"* I screamed. "HOW COULD YOU?" I burst into tears. "*What were you thinking,* Kelly? You were supposed to be my best friend! Ethan! Are you *trying* to hurt me? To ruin our family?"

"Pippa!" Kelly called.

They looked around frantically for their clothes and quickly got dressed as I tromped through the thick leaves of deceit back to my car. My hands were shaking so hard I could barely buckle my seat belt. Ethan and Kelly emerged from the front door and ran toward me as I reversed and backed onto the street. Horns honked as I almost clipped two drivers.

I took one more look at them—half dressed, sex hair—and floored it down the hill. It was one thing to believe your spouse was cheating. It was quite another to see it in the flesh.

And I really needed all my dry cleaning back.

# Thirty-Two

I was having a total breakdown. As soon as I reached Sunset, I pulled into the empty school parking lot, crying, shaking, and quaking.

I felt gutted, like someone had died. I was grieving both my husband and my best friend, or the people I'd thought they were. It was a horrific form of loss.

My sobs slowed to whimpers, and I leaned my head against the seat, finally taking a few calm breaths. Then my phone rang. Josh always seemed to call at these awful moments, or maybe I was just having a lot of awful moments lately. *Should I pick up? Who cared? My life was over.*

"Hello?" I said, sniffling.

"Pippa, it's Josh. I was just calling to confirm my session with—"

"Josh," I said, gulping down tears. "I—I can't—I can't talk right now."

"Are you okay?"

"No," I wailed. "I'm not okay. I'm never going to be okay!"

"What happened?" he asked. "Are you hurt?"

I shook my head, which he couldn't see.

"Where are you? Do you need help?"

I nodded, which he also couldn't see.

"Pippa? Hello?"

"I saw them . . . together . . ."

"Saw who?" Josh asked.

"My husband. And Kelly. My best friend. I saw them. I watched them have *sex*. Through the window. I couldn't tear myself away. It was so awful."

My sobs took over again.

"Oh, Pippa," Josh said softly. "I'm so sorry. What a *prick*. How could he do that to you?"

I shrugged.

"Do you want me to come get you?" he asked. "Where are you?"

I looked around, not even remembering how I'd gotten there.

"I'm in the middle-school parking lot. And I'm still in my pajamas!"

"Oh! I'm here, too!" he said. "I was dropping off homework for one of my students. Hold on, I'm coming outside."

A few minutes later, I heard Josh knocking on my window. My nose was running and my cheeks were wet with tears. Lovely. I grabbed a wad of tissues and motioned for him to go to the passenger side.

"We have to stop meeting like this," he said. "At least this is an upgrade from being on speakerphone."

He sat down beside me silently, his eyes showing so much compassion and care. It was like we were right back at summer camp. I remember when one of the girls in my bunk tore up an art project I'd worked really hard on, the welcome sign for parents' visiting day. Josh had shown up; he'd been there then to give me a hug. Decades had passed, but here he was. Again.

"How could he?" I asked. I felt like Sally in *When Harry Met Sally*, when she realized, "He just didn't want to marry *me*."

"He's an idiot," Josh said. "If you were my wife, man . . ." He shook his head. "I'd make sure every moment of your life was perfect."

I looked up at him with weepy puppy-dog eyes. "You would?"

"Of course," he said. "Anyone would. You're amazing. Why doesn't he see it?"

"I'm not amazing," I said. "I'm a mess! Look at me. *I'm still in my pajamas!*"

"No, you're not a mess," Josh said softly. "And they're very cute pajamas. Plus, you'll save time getting ready for bed tonight. Look at that efficiency. Come on. You're wonderful and you always have been."

I just shook my head as he put his arm around my shoulder over the center console of the car.

"How about we switch seats and I drive you home?" he asked. "I don't think you're in any position to drive."

"How would you get back here?"

"How about this? I'll take you home and then take this car to the shop on my way back. I know the owner of the body shop. I can easily Uber back to my car or get a ride from there."

"What? Why would you do all that for me?"

"It would be my pleasure," he said. "I've been your number-one fan for decades. Plus, it would make me closer to Derek Johnson—another highlight. I can't believe you didn't know who he was!"

*Ugh. Right.* I'd forgotten Josh had been on the phone for *that* whole debacle.

"Thanks, Josh," I said, blowing my nose again.

"Come on, switch with me."

We both got out of the car. My sneakers were soaked from stomping around the Mandeville home. As we crossed at the back of the car, Josh stopped and said, "Can I give you a hug?" There was no motive. I could see it in his face. Josh was just pure sweetness.

I nodded and fell into his arms, crying. I was twelve years old again, back at camp. He stroked my hair softly and whispered, "Shh, shh. It's all going to be okay. It's going to be okay, Pippa."

I didn't know how it would be okay. All I could see was the image of my family, the foundation of everything in my life, cracking and splitting apart, swallowing me up like the opening scene in *Superman*, the earth shape-shifting in front of me. What about the kids? What about our home? What about our life? I was mad at Ethan half the time, yes, but it didn't mean I wanted our marriage to end or our family unit to crumble.

But as Josh comforted me, I had the slightest feeling that maybe things would someday be okay again.

# Thirty-Three

As Josh drove me home, his arm casually draped over the back of my seat, I played out what I *thought* my life was going to bring. It was time to scrub out all future memories with Ethan: driving Zoe to college as a family, Passover dinners with both of our crazy mothers, growing old and (probably not) grayer together, that trip to Italy we never took. All of it. Gone.

Why did Ethan do it? With *Kelly* of all people? And why was he always so *angry* at me? Why did I just grin and bear it?

Part of me knew that I'd never get satisfying answers. I mean, why does anyone do anything? And in the end, did it even matter? Was it Ethan's early success as a child actor? Did it make him unable to operate in a layperson's world? Was he just . . . a bad person? Could that be it? I liked to believe that bad people didn't exist, that if I could just talk to someone, they'd like me and want the best for me like I wanted the best for everyone else. But maybe it was as simple as that.

As for Kelly, that was another story.

She'd been my ride or die for decades. There was no excuse. None. That heartbreak was far more painful. Relationships, even marriage, could change. But best friends? There was no substitute.

Josh pulled into my driveway.

"Okay," he said, talking to me like I was one of his students, "you go inside. Maybe even get dressed! I'll take the car to the repair shop.

And I'll be back tonight for Max's tutoring and dinner, if you still want me to come."

"Yes, yes, tonight, right," I said. "I'll pull myself together by then. I promise."

He smiled and rubbed my back. "Hey, you don't have to pull yourself together for me."

"I'll be with the kids. I don't want them to find out what happened."

"What are you going to do when Ethan comes home?"

"I have no idea. I . . . I need to . . . I don't know. Find a lawyer? I'll call my mom. I know she has people who can help me."

"Okay. Good. Call your mom. Tell you what: I'll also pick up Max from school today in my car. Give you a little rest. All good."

"Thanks, Josh. That would be great, actually. I know Zoe already has a ride back. I'll call the school and let them know."

"No problem. On it! You sure you're okay?"

I nodded. "Yes—I mean, no, I'm not okay at all. But I can manage. I'll handle it."

"You got this, Pippa," Josh said as I got out of the car. "I'll see you soon."

I stood and watched him drive away until I could only hear the faint sound of my messed-up Volvo chugging around the corner.

*Now what?* I headed upstairs to change and call my mom.

"It's over," I said when she picked up.

"What's over?" she asked. "Seymour! Turn down the music. It's Pippa. What's over, dear?"

"My marriage. I saw Ethan cheating on me today. With Kelly. I saw the whole thing."

"Gross," she said. "Pippa, what an image! Those middle-aged schlubs."

"Mom, what are you talking about? You're, like, a senior citizen at this point."

"But I'm still gorgeous. A catch! Ethan and Kelly—blech. Seymour, tell her! How smokin' am I?"

"Like a barbecue in summer!" Seymour yelled back.

"Mom . . . please."

"Like a fire in an Aspen lodge!" he added. "Like an onion volcano at a Benihana!"

"Okay, please tell Seymour thank you for that. I get it."

"I couldn't stand that guy anyway. He was never any good to you. Seymour, my love, grab the dogs! We're going to LA right now. Let's go, let's go! Start the car!" I could hear her shoes clacking on the tile foyer as she raced around. "Pippa, we're on our way."

"Thanks, Mom. I'm sorry."

"Canasta can wait. I always want more time with those grandchildren."

"Mom? Thank you. It means a lot."

She sighed. "Pippa, I know I wasn't the best mother. I'm not sure if I knew how to be. But I love you, dear heart. And if driving through the desert when your husband royally F's up shows you in ways I couldn't years ago, then good. I just need to be back in time for bridge tomorrow at two p.m. Seymour, did you get the dogs?!"

"Got the dogs!"

I laughed. If nothing else, the visit would be a welcome distraction.

Now there was just one more call I had to make. I couldn't face Josie and Gabriela yet. But Kelly. I had to know: *Why?*

# Thirty-Four

Ding!

As I waited for my mom and Seymour to arrive—and for Josh to get back—my phone blew up with listing alerts. *Open house! New build with designer fixtures, professionally decorated, move-in ready. Infinity pool.*

Wait, what was *that* one?! Not only was the home gorgeous in the photos, but it was just down the block from us. I'd been watching the construction carefully over the past couple of years, but it had been like Fort Knox over there. The developers hadn't let in a soul; apparently they'd had all workers sign waivers so they couldn't discuss any of the designer features until the house went on the market.

Who knew that today would be the day?

I had to go see it—Kelly could wait. Maybe today I'd even go in without a costume. This wasn't for the Instagram account; it was just for me.

I walked down the hill to get to the house. Being without a car allowed me to see all the details: the new flower beds my neighbor Isabelle had planted, the beautiful palm trees lining the way, the fresh coat of paint on our other neighbor Genevieve's fence. All the little things that I normally overlooked in my rush to get from one place to the next. Maybe the mess of my life was a sign for me to slow down.

And then: the house! I stood on the curb and took in the details. The modern construction, floor-to-ceiling windows, reclaimed-wood garage door, winding driveway, manicured lawn. As I admired the construction from the front curb, another car drove up, a giant Escalade. And from the backseat, out hopped someone dolled up and put together. A tiny fireball of a woman with a heaping ponytail of blonde hair. Maybe a reality star?

As she passed, I gave her a little smile.

WAIT.

Was it?

"Are you . . . Ella Rankin?"

She stopped and turned around.

"Yes?"

"Oh my gosh, I'm such a fan. I'm Pippa Jones," I said, extending my hand for a shake. "I'm also an author, but not like you or anything."

"Oh, Pippa! I loved *Poppies*!" she said, walking over. She stretched out her hand and my eyes welled up with tears.

"Was my handshake that bad?" Ella pulled back and looked me in the eye, clearly concerned as I shook my head. "You okay?"

"I'm sorry. I'm sorry," I sniffled, waving my hand to dismiss the seriousness. "This is so embarrassing. Just having some issues today. My marriage . . ."

"Hey, aren't you doing that *Blank* book?"

"You heard about it?"

"Sure. I read the industry news like everyone else. It's been hard to miss! Hold on a sec." She motioned to her driver, who rolled down the front window.

"What's up, boss?" he asked, his bald head gleaming, a boyish grin on his face.

"I'm going to be here for a little while," she said. "Meet me back here in, say, an hour?"

He gave her a thumbs-up and said, "You got it." Then he smiled at me and drove off.

"He's *so* nice," Ella said. "Should we check out the house? You can tell me all about your marriage woes. I love a good story." She linked her arm in mine. "So are you looking at the house for fun, or are you moving, or what?"

"For fun mostly," I said. "You?"

"Oh, I love open houses," she said. "I follow this amazing Instagram account, @openhousebandit. You have to check it out. It's a hoot and shows everything new. Do you follow it?"

I laughed. "Intimately."

"Well, let's get in there!"

As we waited for the broker to open the door, I decided to go for it.

"Hey, Ella?" I said. "I know this is going to sound nuts. But when you announced your book *Podlusters*, I'd literally been writing a book with the exact same title and plot. I'd thought of it when I was on vacation in Hawaii and my friend Gabriela told me she wanted to meet the bookstagram guy @underthehardcovers. And then I saw you on TV announcing your book . . . and had to toss out almost two hundred pages."

"Oh gosh, ouch!" she said. "I don't even like to delete words if it means it'll take longer to hit my word count."

"If you don't mind my asking, how *did* you come up with the idea? Do you even remember?"

She took a deep breath. "Okay, I gotta be honest here. I had help. I was at the Miami Book Fair and during my panel, I mentioned that I couldn't think of a good idea for my next novel. After I finished, a fan came over and said she had the most amazing idea ever. I was like, 'Yes, darlin'! That's what I need!' So she told me some of it and then asked me to pay her an upfront fee for the whole thing. And unlike most terrible ideas—I'm sure you know that *everyone* has a book idea, right?—this one was solid gold. I *loved* it. Loved it!

"So I paid her what she asked and that was that. I asked her if she was totally okay with my using it, and she said as long as I didn't tell anyone that I hadn't thought of it myself, then it'd be fine. It seemed like a fine trade-off. Made me look smarter, that's for sure.

"So I went on back home and whipped it out in just a couple months, sent it to my editor, and we published it quickly. They require one book a year from me now, and boy, I have trouble cranking out fiction that fast. My whole life has to stop, you know?! One book a year plus all that marketing and publicity is intense. I need all the help I can get!"

The door opened.

"Welcome, ladies!" A peppy, wire-thin real estate broker greeted us with a giant smile. She wore huge sunglasses on top of her ringlet-filled head. "I'm Melody. Let me know if you need anything!"

"Wow!" Ella said, looking around.

The home was straight out of *Architectural Digest*. Giant wood beams on a pale-blue lacquered ceiling. Reclaimed-wood floors. Beautiful large-scale photographs on the wall. Plants and fresh flowers, artfully arranged. A sitting area in front of a fireplace.

"Well, we're just gonna plop ourselves down right here and talk for a few minutes," Ella told Melody. "Okay with you?"

"Well, we do have a number of showings lined up," she stumbled.

"Great," Ella said. "We'll be quick about it."

I laughed.

"Never take no for an answer," she whispered, touching my hand.

We sank into the deepest, plushest couch ever, both of us saying, "Ahh!" as Melody raced off to answer the door for the next potential clients.

"Ella, what did she look like?" I asked. "The fan. Do you remember? Do you remember her name? Anything about her?"

"Well, she was just adorable. White-blonde hair. Real little but strong-looking. Maybe shoulder-length hair? I can't remember too much else. I never even got her name! I do recall that she was wearing a hat and sunglasses, which I remember thinking was odd since it was a rainy afternoon, one of those Florida storms."

"Would you recognize her again?"

"Maybe. Why?"

I pulled out my phone and found an old photo of Kelly and me. "Is this her?"

"For heaven's sake! Yes, that's her! Gosh, I need to thank her! Are you two friends?"

"We were," I said, putting my head in my hands.

*Oh my god.*

Kelly.

She'd deliberately destroyed my life. In more ways than one.

But *why*?

———

From the upstairs bedroom with the wraparound terrace, I called Gabriela and Josie for a double FaceTime while Ella checked out the walk-in closets.

"What's up, Pips?" Josie asked. "I only have two minutes before I go back on air."

"I'm about to go riding," Gabriela said. "You okay?"

"I am *not* okay. Listen, you have to keep this to yourselves right now. You won't believe it." I took a deep, deep breath.

"This morning, I saw Kelly having sex with Ethan. My Ethan. Don't even ask how I knew where they were. More on that later. And *now* I just found out from Ella Rankin herself that Kelly gave her the idea for *Podlusters*. And I'm guessing it was Kelly who told the reporters where to find Zoe and Max, too."

"Kelly?" Gabriela said. "*Our* Kelly? Couldn't be."

Josie added, "Are you sure? Pippa, did you take anything new? Pain medication or a gummy that's making you hallucinate? This sounds bananas."

"I'm sure. I saw them with my own eyes, and *that's* a sight I'll never forget. I know it's all crazy. But no, I'm not on drugs. I've only stopped crying because I'm so frickin' angry. Listen, did either of you know about Ethan and Kelly? Or about Kelly telling Ella? Be honest. I don't know who to trust anymore, and if we're all cutting ties and I'm losing friends, I'd prefer to do it all at once."

"Whoa, whoa, don't throw us under the bus," Gabriela said. "But, well . . . Kelly did tell me she had taken a lover, but not who he was. She told me not to tell anyone. Of course, if I'd known it was *Ethan*, I would have told you, my love!"

"I didn't know a *thing*," Josie said. "I can put our investigative team on it if you want. And, Pippa? Lady, I am so sorry."

"Thanks. Yeah, my life is pretty much over."

"Maybe not," Josie said. "Maybe it's about to get a whole lot better?"

"I highly doubt that."

"I wonder if Arthur knows," Josie added. "Should we tell him?"

"I'm going to call Kelly," Gabriela said. "How could she do this?"

"Please don't—not yet. I'm working on it."

# Thirty-Five

Sometimes you just can't trust men," Ella said.

"Or women," I added.

Ella and I were walking back to my house after the tour. I'd invited her over for Shabbat dinner with Josh and whoever else showed up. She'd actually never been to a Shabbat meal before. I was excited to show her how delicious and meaningful a family meal with challah and wine on a Friday night could be.

Yet Ella and I also had more in common than I could have imagined. Turns out she was also struggling with the impact of fame on her writing. *And* she'd been propositioned by Michael, too. That's why she'd decided to publish with Troubadour: it was run by women. Ella said she'd be honored to blurb and promote *Blank*.

"Oh, isn't this block lovely!" she said as we got to my home.

"That one's mine," I said, pointing to our house.

"No way!"

Just as we were about to climb the steps to the front porch, a car pulled up. We both turned to look. I gasped and grabbed Ella's arm.

*No. Seriously?* It was Ethan and Kelly. TOGETHER. In his car. Coming to our house. *How dare they?*

"It's them," I whispered.

"No!" Ella said. "The *nerve*."

Anger overtook me. "I'm going to bash in that windshield," I said, peeling away from Ella toward the car.

"Um, Pippa? This isn't one of our novels. Now, you come right back here before you do something foolish."

Before I could go a step farther, Josh pulled up with Max. Then Zoe popped out of a giant pickup driven by a dark and handsome teen who definitely was *not* Greta. It was like a parking lot in my driveway. As they all got out of their cars, I could see Max glance at Zoe's mystery driver, taking in his sleeve of tattoos. He walked up to me, motioned to the driver, and said, "Well, he's not getting buried in a Jewish cemetery."

"Yes, *that* is definitely her," Ella whispered, pointing at Kelly.

"Great. Just great," I said.

I walked over and hugged Zoe and Max in close.

"Hi, Aunt Kelly!" Max said.

"She's not Aunt Kelly anymore," I said, glaring in her direction.

"Oh yeah? Uncle Kelly? I'm cool with that, too," Zoe said.

"She's not your aunt or your uncle. She's nothing to us anymore."

Zoe ignored me, stepped forward, and said, "Kelly, I can be your nibling!"

"Her what?!" Ella said.

"Everyone," I called, "this is Ella Rankin."

"What?!" Zoe exclaimed. "*The* Ella Rankin?"

"The one and only, at your service," she answered, curtsying a little.

Max pointed a finger at her. "You're the one who stole *Podlusters*!"

"Hey buddy, I didn't steal it. I didn't know it was someone else's," Ella said. "Your little uncle Kelly over there gave me the idea. Yep. Gave it right to me and told me not to tell anyone it wasn't my own."

"What?" Ethan said. He turned to Kelly. "Is that true?"

"Aunt Kelly? Did you do that to Mom?" Zoe asked, horrified.

Kelly couldn't even look at us. She and Ethan, still by their car in the pileup, looked at each other, and then Kelly stood looking down at the ground as the rest of us stared at her in a semicircle.

"How could you do that to Pippa?" Josh asked, putting his arm around me.

"Wait, who are you?" Ethan asked.

"I'm Max's new bar mitzvah tutor. I went to camp with your wife."

"Oh my god, wait. Are you Deodorant Guy?" Zoe asked, covering her mouth and giggling.

"No, but I was good friends with Deodorant Guy," Josh answered. "I taught him everything he knew. And he introduced me to your mom at a dance."

"Ewwww!" said Max, laughing.

"Do you see me sweating now?" Josh replied, gesturing to his own face. "Eh?! Maybe I was on to something!"

I took a few steps toward Kelly. "How *could* you?" I asked her. "*Why?* All of it. The book. Ethan. We were best friends."

"What do you mean *all of it*, Mom?" Zoe asked. "What *about* Dad?"

Ella nudged Josh. "Oh, this is gonna be good," she said.

I nodded toward Ethan. "Maybe you should ask your father."

"Dad?" Max walked over to Ethan. "What's going on?"

Ethan and Kelly just stood there, as if trying to decide what to say.

"No," Zoe said as it slowly dawned on her what was happening.

"No, what?" Max said, innocently.

Ethan cleared his throat. "Kelly and I . . ."

Max turned to ask me again. "What?"

Ethan cleared his throat. "Kelly and I have started a romantic relationship."

Silence.

Max looked at Ethan and then back at me. "Is this a joke or something?"

I shook my head. "I wish," I said. "I found out yesterday."

"What?" Max said to Ethan, his hands raised in the air. "You can't have another romantic relationship! You're married to Mom! Kelly's her best friend! That's not how it's supposed to work!"

Then Max turned to me: "You said you weren't getting divorced!"

"Well, love, I wasn't planning on it."

"This wasn't my plan either, bud," Ethan said.

Max stuck out his chest and stood up as straight as possible. "Don't. Call. Me. Bud." Then he moved closer to me and hugged me tight around my middle.

"I . . . I don't even know where to start," Kelly said.

Just then yet another car pulled up. *WTF?!* Michael, the two pony-tail girls, and Rodger the lawyer piled out. *I mean, seriously. Who drives this far for a meeting in Los Angeles?!*

I walked over to the Escalade. "Michael, what are *you* doing here?"

Michael tucked in his white V-neck, smoothed out his hair, and looked around.

"Nice place," he noted. "So, we heard from the Ella Rankin team that intellectual property theft occurred on the premises. We'll need to talk to Kelly Chambers."

"Oh my god," Kelly said.

Ella and I exchanged a quick glance.

"Helloooo! I'm right over here," Ella said, her hands on her hips. "That was me."

"Wow," said Josh. "Way to act quickly."

Brittany suddenly emerged from the back of the SUV. "We thought this whole story would make for great PR. Don't mind me. I'm just snapping a few pics." She gave me a big thumbs-up sign with a secret smile and mouthed, "Yes!"

"I need a lawyer," Kelly said.

"Looks like I have one," I said, smiling. "Thanks for having my back, Michael. And Rodger."

Rodger gave me a salute.

"I told you—I *see* you," Michael said. He turned to Kelly. "And now? Spill it, darlin'. What'd you do?"

Kelly shook her head.

"Hold on, hold on!" I said. "I'm FaceTiming Josie and Gabriela. They can't miss this."

I got them both on split screen, and slowly Kelly started talking. Not sure why; she should've known better than to spontaneously spill her guts, especially after months (years?!) of secrets and lies. But maybe the authority of the legal counsel unnerved her enough to just blab?

"I'm—I'm sorry," she said. "I . . . I couldn't tell anyone what was really going on in my life, so I just started meddling with someone else's, thinking mine wouldn't seem so bad. It sounds really bad when I say it out loud. But I didn't mean to hurt anybody."

"Just really bad?" I said. "That would be generous."

"I haven't told anyone this," Kelly continued, "but Arthur has been in jail for insider trading for the past two years. He's being punished for his financial malfeasance. That's why he hasn't been around lately. Didn't you notice he never came to any industry galas? I always said he was busy or working, but really, yes—he has been in jail. That's why he doesn't show up to dinner parties."

"Now, that's a good excuse," Ethan said, chuckling.

I just shook my head. "Sorry."

"We lost absolutely everything. I couldn't even afford the kids' schools. And I was too ashamed to tell anyone."

"Kelly! We would've been there for you," I said. "We've been best friends for decades. We all could've helped! Instead you went and ruined my life."

Kelly hung her head. "The kids have been going to P.S. 139. How could I admit that to anyone?! *Public school?* In *Manhattan*! I guess I needed to bring others down with me. I don't know what I was thinking. I was desperate. Then I secretly sold our apartment; we definitely can't afford it anymore. We're living in a one bedroom. On First Avenue!"

"Is now when we're supposed to feel sorry for you?" Ella asked, catching my eye.

Kelly nodded. "And with *no help*."

I just gave her a blank stare. We didn't have any hired help either, if that's what she meant. Were we seriously supposed to feel sorry for her?

"Never mind," she said. "It just . . . hasn't been easy. But at least I made some money from *HighJILLed*, so we could still afford food, medical care, and all the necessities. And that's when I started selling book ideas. Some of mine. Some of Gabriela's. Some of yours," she said, pointing at me with her chin.

"Is this all true, Aunt Kelly?" Zoe asked. "It sounds made-up."

"Yes, Zo. I'm so sorry."

"I didn't know the full story," Ethan admitted.

"And, Pippa," Kelly said, turning to me. "I don't know. I was just so upset. And you were always complaining about not being able to write and yet coming up with masterpieces, living in your nice home with your brand-new office and movie-star husband, and I was just insanely jealous.

"And when you told me about *Podlusters*, I didn't think you would actually *write* it. You think of twenty-seven book ideas a *day*, and I'm lucky if I think of one a year—and then I have to write it as fast as possible while dealing with the logistics of the kids. It's, like, impossible. My writing income has been exclusively supporting us—which, of course, isn't enough for the crazy-expensive Upper East Side. So, I don't know. I needed to bring in funds some other way."

I wasn't totally buying it. "But why didn't you tell us about Arthur?"

"I was just too ashamed," she continued. "It was awful. And as for Ethan . . ."

"Yeah," I said. "If you could explain that one . . ."

She looked at him guiltily.

"Don't you dare," he growled.

She bit her lip.

"I wouldn't threaten her if I were you," Michael said, puffing up his waxed chest.

"Kids," I said, "go inside."

Josh had been looking around uncomfortably. "I'll take them in," he said in a hurry. "Come on, Max, Zoe . . ."

"I'm not moving a muscle," Max said. "If this is about my dad, I need to know."

"Well," Kelly began, "Ethan offered to take care of my money problems if I would just . . ."

Zoe prodded. "What? If you would just *what*?!"

"Pippa, I was desperate," Kelly said. "I needed the cash. I know it's horrible, but I thought my life was over. It was either saying yes to Ethan and living out whatever fantasies he had, or dying by suicide, which I thought about literally every single day. The only reason I didn't was because I couldn't bear putting that shame on my kids. But some days I thought they'd be better off without me."

I shook my head.

"How did Ethan even know you needed money?" Rodger, the lawyer, interjected.

"Well," Kelly said, "remember when I came out here for the hardcover release of *The JILLson Five*?"

I flashed back to the time when Kelly came to town just for the night and Ethan and I took her to dinner at the Polo Lounge at the Beverly Hills Hotel. All I really remember was her ordering her food with no oil, no carbs, and something else that made me think, "Why even order the dish?! Have a bowl of lettuce and call it a day." Had she and Ethan snuck away without me? Were they passing notes under the table? I'm certain I wasn't up from my seat for more than a few minutes. Did anything happen during the signing?

"Yeah, I remember," I said. "Sort of . . ."

"Well," Kelly explained, "I came to the house the next morning to chat with you about your book, confess about Arthur, and all of it, but you were out somewhere. Ethan didn't know where. Some school meeting or something."

"Some school meeting he was supposed to be at, too? Okay, continue." I held up my hand. "And, wait—that was like a full year ago."

"Yeah," Kelly said. "Thirteen months, actually. Anyway, Ethan told me he thought *you* were having an affair because you were always slinking off in the middle of the day. *Were you*, by the way? Let's come back to that."

"I was not. *Am* not," I said. "Don't have to come back to it."

"So I confided to Ethan what happened to Arthur. But I promise, he didn't know about *Podlusters*."

"Yeah, I actually can't believe you did that," Ethan said.

"Oh, so now you have a conscience?" Kelly snapped at him. He shut right up. I glanced at Josh, who gave me a sympathetic shrug. "He's the only person I told about the depths of our financial despair. And he suggested a solution. He'd pay for my parents to come to New York to take care of the kids and would rent me a private home in LA where I could work on my books uninterrupted. The only stipulation was that when he . . . wanted something . . . I had to stop what I was doing to . . . you know."

"I don't know," I said.

She started making spinning movements with her hand.

"Churn butter?"

"No. Have . . ."

I whipped around. "ETHAN. You were paying my best friend for . . . ?!" I resorted to the butter-churning motion, too, trying not to let the kids know that their father had made my best friend a prostitute.

"DAD!" Max yelled.

"Dad?" Zoe burst into tears. "How could you?"

"And you took the money, Kelly?" Gabriela asked over the phone. "How could you do that?"

"I didn't think I had a choice."

"I think you'd better leave," Josh said, stepping toward Ethan.

"This is my house," Ethan said.

"Not for long," I snapped.

Rodger stepped in front of me. "Ethan, my advice is that you get a lawyer, pronto."

"Dad, I never want to see you again for the rest of my life!" Max yelled and then ran into the house.

"Max!" Zoe said, running after him and then calling over her shoulder, "Seriously, Dad. Could you be any more of a douchebag?! What the hell?"

"And, Kelly," Rodger continued, "you're going to need to retain counsel, too, for intellectual property theft, among other things."

"I can't believe this is happening," I said.

"This is so good," Brittany said, still snapping away with her iPhone.

Ethan held up his arm and threw his blazer around Kelly. "Come on. Cut it out. No photos. I'll be back later to see the kids. Kelly, let's go."

"Oh, don't bother coming back," I said.

Kelly and Ethan climbed into his car.

My heart broke for Zoe and Max. How could he betray *their* trust, too? How on earth was I going to handle this? The kids were going to be a mess. My family was imploding. And it wasn't even time to light the Shabbat candles yet.

As I reeled from the aftermath of the showdown, Brittany actually started clapping. "Oh yeah. We're going to milk these pics for all they're worth and get you what you de*serve*."

Ella spun around to face me. "Well, silver lining: I don't think you or I will ever have a problem coming up with a book idea again," she said. "I've thought of sixteen different novels just based on this scene alone."

"And how did you get involved in all this, may I ask?" Michael asked Ella.

She marched over to him and crossed her arms across her chest. "Michael, you've propositioned me about five different times. I have a stash of key cards from you sitting in my desk at home. You really don't think I should be *involved*?"

Michael turned beet red.

Ella whirled around and addressed the already stunned crowd in my driveway.

"Yep. This man has propositioned every author with a skirt and somehow gotten away with it. He has used and abused his power to further his own career. And I don't think we need to put up with this anymore."

"Woo-hooooo!" Josie cheered from FaceTime. "I got key cards, too!"

"Me, too," I said.

"But, but . . ." Michael started.

"But nothing," Ella said, her arms crossed. "And guess what? *We see you*, too."

Rodger put his hand on Michael's shoulder. "In my expert opinion, you better get the hell out of here before you dig an even deeper hole for yourself," he advised.

"Fine," Michael barked, glaring at me. "But this won't be the end of it."

Michael, Rodger, and, seemingly reluctantly, Brittany, got back in the Escalade, where the ponytail girls were waiting with who-knows-what on the rocks in crystal glasses for Michael. We saw him take one swig as he sat down. Ella gave him the "I'm watching you" gesture, like Robert De Niro in *Meet the Parents*. Michael slammed the door and the car peeled away.

Holy crap. Was all this really happening? Ella Rankin was at my house, saving the day.

"Oh my GOD, you were *amazing*, Ella!" I said, giving her a huge hug.

Josh just shook his head. "Man, you should be a prosecutor," he said.

"Oh, I think being a novelist is *way* more fun," Ella retorted. "Is it time for cocktails yet? This has been one heck of an afternoon. Is this what it's always like in the neighborhood? I might have to come here more often."

Later, with the help of a much-needed cocktail, Ella posted a photo of me surrounded by all the driveway commotion on Instagram: *Author of the upcoming book Blank gets her own action! This book is NOT to be missed. #bff #newfriend.*

A public spectacle. My private pain.

Just as we were about to light the candles at dinner—and yes, I ended up making chicken nuggets again to go with the challah and wine—I heard a loud noise from the foyer. Was Ethan sneaking in?

Nope. If only.

My mother and Seymour stood inside the front door in a swirling cloud of desert sand. She was holding a giant floppy hat and the leashes of her barking dogs, who were jumping up her legs. He was carrying the twenty-seven tote bags they'd packed.

As if the day hadn't been dramatic enough.

"We're *here*!" my mom exclaimed, arms outstretched, eyes to the ceiling. "Let the healing begin." She paraded through the house in her floor-length caftan and high heels, her hair in a chignon, bright-red lipstick slathered on her thin lips. "Seymour, park the car and bring in the dog food. Now, where are my precious grandchildren?"

Max and Zoe giggled.

"Right here, Gee-Gee," Max said.

"No, come on. My grandchildren are *babies*! Who could you be?" she joked. (I hoped.)

"We grew up," Max said.

"You can say that again!"

"We grew up," he repeated.

"This is the comedian, eh?" she said, pinching his cheeks. "Come on, let's say the prayers so I can start drinking wine. You didn't start the Shabbat celebration without us, right? Of course not." It wasn't until we all went inside the house that I realized she hadn't even said hello to me.

"And who might you be," she said, linking arms with Josh.

Josh glanced back at me and smiled.

*Here we go.*

*Amen.*

# Thirty-Six

Brittany got her wish. The social media blitz of our driveway scene spiked preorders of *Blank* to five hundred thousand by the end of dinner, and I hadn't written a word. To augment her informal footage, Brittany drafted an official press release, which she'd send out the next day. My phone was blowing up. By dessert, I'd received three movie offers and a book deal for my life rights.

After we'd cleaned up, putting the challah remnants in a baggie for French toast the next morning ("Wait, there are *other* kinds of French toast besides challah?" my daughter had recently asked), I beckoned to Ella and Josh to look at the insanity of my inbox.

"Don't make any hasty decisions," Ella said as she and I skimmed through bold names on my phone.

Then I heard a loud knock.

"Hey lady! Let me in!"

"Josie?!"

I opened the front door. Josie rushed through it and pulled me in tightly, her long, lean limbs enveloping me like she was the envelope to my old-school letter.

"You came!" I said as we hugged.

"I couldn't let you go through all this alone!"

We pulled apart and smiled at each other. "But what about the show?" I asked her. "You're going to miss work!"

She batted the air. "The show can wait. And who knows, maybe you and I could do a one-on-one interview someday and really knock the socks off my producers. If they wear socks . . . You know what I mean."

I laughed. "So happy you're here." I motioned to Josh. "And Josie, meet Josh."

Josh shook her hand and grinned. "Nice to meet you."

"You look like a good dude," she said. "I can see it in your eyes. Bring it in for a hug."

"You can thank my parents for those," Josh said as they hugged like old friends.

"I could use a Scotch," Josie said.

"I drank it all!" my mom yelled from the other room.

Josie raised an eyebrow.

"Yeah," I said, "my mom and Seymour are here. They've only been here a couple hours and already decided to head home after dinner."

"Maybe that's for the best?" Josie said.

"Want some tequila on the rocks?" my mom called from the bar. "I'm pouring!"

Josie laughed. "Sure!"

"How many nights can you stay, Jo?" I turned to the kids. "Max and Zoe, can you share a room tonight while Josie's here?"

"Sure. Can Josh stay over, too?" Max asked, sheepishly. "I'd feel a lot better if he were here. What if Dad comes back?"

"Me, too," Zoe said.

"You two *literally* just met Josh this week," I said.

"It's been a crazy week," said Max.

Josie plopped down on the couch, shook off her high heels, and crossed her outstretched legs on the ottoman. "Well, I'm staying as long as you need me to."

"Me, too!" Ella added, appearing suddenly. "Sorry, I was just checking out the rooms upstairs. What a nice view!"

"It's not for sale," I said with a wink.

"I know, I know. But I'm always looking." She turned to Josie. "Ella Rankin, nice to meet you."

"Another hug," Josie said, towering over her.

"Bring it in!"

Ella and Josie hugged as the kids exchanged a look.

"Josh, you can stay in my room," Max offered. "I'm happy to stay with Zoe. Josie can stay in the guest room."

"That's so nice of you, buddy," Josh said. "Is that okay with your mom?"

Everyone looked at me.

I didn't even know which way was up. I'd been deceived, duped, and defriended. And yet somehow I was feeling celebratory surrounded by my crazy family, Josie, my old camp buddy. My chosen people.

"Sure. Why not?"

"Yes!" Max said, fist pumping the air.

"I'd be happy to," Josh said. "I just need to go back home and get Dayenu—if he's welcome, too? We're kind of a package deal."

"Sure. Of course. Bring Dayenu," I said. *Dayenu*. The prayer meant: *It would have been enough.* I looked at him, then at the group. "If Josh had just helped with Max's lockdown . . ."

"Dayenu!" they yelled.

"If Josh had just helped with Max's lockdown but not gotten my car fixed . . ."

"Dayenu!"

"If Josh had just gotten my car fixed but not picked up Max at school . . ."

"Dayenu!"

"If Josh had just picked up Max at school but not helped us all night . . ."

"Dayenu!"

I turned to Josh. All of us were laughing.

"If Josh had been wonderful to my kids but not been so wonderful to me . . ."

"Dayenu!"

It almost felt normal at home. Ethan was usually gone anyway.

"This is too much," my mom said. "What is this? The Palisades choir? Seymour, time to go. Grab the dogs. Pippa is fine here. She doesn't need us."

"Mom—"

"You called? I came. You're good? I leave." She headed for the front door.

"Mom, where are you rushing back to?" I asked as she grabbed her hat and totes.

"We have our whole lives in the desert, dear. Marty Shaeffer is hosting poker night. We can catch the end of it."

My mom flitted around, air-kissing everyone goodbye. I just shook my head. She caught sight of me, grabbed my chin, and said, "Listen to your mother: *no more losers*. You hear? Keep that Hebrew guy around. He seems nice. And don't forget to get your highlights done. You're grayer than I am!"

I laughed. "Okay, Mom. Got it."

"Good. Max and Zoe, stop growing! Enough already. Stay babies. Josie, Josh, Ella, everyone, be well!" And with that, she sauntered out the door and to the car, Seymour behind her, pulling the dogs along.

*If they had just visited after more than forty days and forty nights in the desert . . .*

*Dayenu.*

# Thirty-Seven

I knocked lightly on Max's door until Josh answered, wearing just his boxers and T-shirt. Dayenu snuggled on the foot of Max's bed.

"Oh wow, sorry. I just wanted to see if you needed a towel or anything," I said.

Josh laughed.

"I didn't exactly pack for vacation," he said. "Looks like Dayenu approves."

"This might be the most bizarre day of my entire life," I said. "I don't even know how to begin processing any of it. But thank you. Thank you for being here. For me. And for Max. Even Zoe. Everyone."

We stood in the doorframe, smiling.

"It's *tikkun olam*. A good deed. It's what we're all here to do."

My heart fluttered a bit. I thought it had been stomped into smithereens, but maybe some part of it had stayed intact?

"I want to be here for you guys. Seriously," he said. "I'm not happy about *how* we reconnected, but I'm really happy we did."

"Me, too," I whispered, suddenly shy as I looked up at him.

And then, as if in a rom-com, we slowly, slowly, inched toward each other until we were softly kissing—Max's old Legos on the shelf behind us, Dayenu's front paws suddenly on Josh's back.

"Breaking news!" Josie called out from down the hall. "Jilted wife and betrayed friend gets some nookie. Where's the camera crew?!"

We pulled away and laughed.

"I was just getting the door for another special visitor," Josie said.

"Another visitor?" I asked. "I don't know if I can take one more surprise. I need to go to bed!"

"I'm he-ere!"

I heard an unmistakable voice. "Gaby?!"

Josie opened the front door, and there she was, Gabriela—her hair blown out, clad in a tight cashmere sweater with a Hermès scarf around her neck and tan pants with knee-high brown leather boots.

"Where are you going? To a Ralph Lauren photo shoot?" I asked, hugging her.

"Ah, my friend. I am so sorry about Ethan. About Kelly. I cannot be*lieve* it."

"She's over it," Josie said matter-of-factly as she carried in Gabriela's bags. "Already making out with that guy." She gestured toward Josh.

"Thanks for the lovely introduction," he said to Josie, extending his hand to Gabriela. "I'm Josh."

"Max's bar mitzvah tutor and Pippa's old camp friend," Josie said. "We all caught up now? I'm going to get ready for bed."

Ella walked over to Gabriela, too. "And I'm Ella Rankin. I know—*Podlusters*. We're over it."

"It's lovely to meet you," Gabriela said, smiling. "Bed? No! Drinks? Yes!"

"This day is just *not* gonna end," Josie said, shaking her head. "But okay. One more drink. Let's do it."

"Be right there," I said, grinning and hugging Gabriela again. "I can't believe you came."

"I thought you were going to be upset. To be honest, maybe I wouldn't have flown across this whole country if I'd known you were already over what happened and together with someone else. I thought you'd be distraught, inconsolable!"

"I think in some ways this whole thing has been a relief," I said. "Not with Kelly; that betrayal has been just horrific. But maybe I'm relieved that my issues with Ethan are now out in the open."

"Very, very open," Gabriela said, kissing my cheek.

Josie and Gabriela went to the kitchen as I walked Josh back to Max's bedroom. I gave him a huge hug, and as I pulled back, we kissed again, slowly and sweetly at first. Then he led me into the bedroom and closed the door, kissing me with more urgency. He pressed me up against the wall and stroked my body like it was a sacred object, his hands lightly caressing my waist.

*Oh my god.*

My legs were weak. My heart was pounding. I hadn't been kissed in years—and I'd *never* been kissed like this. I didn't want it to stop.

Josh took a step back and held my chin, angling my face as if inspecting it closely.

"You are the most beautiful woman alive," he said. "I can't believe I get to kiss you."

"Don't *ever* stop kissing me, please," I said.

"Deal," he said.

Someone knocked on the door.

Gabriela called out, "Seriously? Stop making out! I came all this way to see you!"

"Oh, you're one to talk, Gaby." I pulled away from Josh, smoothed out my hair, and almost opened the door before he pulled me to him again.

"Good night, beautiful," he said, kissing me on my forehead, then my eyelids, then both cheeks and my lips.

"Good night," I whispered, kissing him back, and biting his lower lip just a smidge.

"Mmm, I like that move," Josh said. "If she had just kissed me . . ."

"Dayenu," I whispered.

"If she had just kissed me but not done that cool move . . ."

"Dayenu!"

I walked out the door and he shut it behind me. I realized I was grinning ear to ear, and I let out a huge sigh.

Gabriela and I walked downstairs together and met Josie at the kitchen island, which was covered in liquor bottles and half-filled glasses—the remnants of the night with my mom, Ella, and the rest of the crew.

"So that was something," Josie said.

"Something? Oh my gosh, I haven't felt like that in ages," I whispered, wiping my brow. "Sheesh. I need a fan. Is it hot in here or is it just me?"

"Menopause meets Mr. Perfect," Josie said.

The three of us laughed. But then I had a surge of anxiety.

"I'm going to be okay, right?" I asked. "This is somehow all going to work out?"

"Yes, we're *all* gonna be okay," Gabriela said.

"The kids, too?" I asked. "What do you think? I'm so worried. It was a lot for them today."

Josie said, "Can't vouch for them."

I sighed.

Josie pointed at Gabriela. "Are you still canoodling with your trainer, Gaby?"

She nodded, taking a sip of wine.

"And Juan Carlos doesn't know?" I asked.

Gabriela shook her head. "Ah, he knows. And now he's with our nanny. It's crazy, right? But it works for us." She smiled and shrugged. "And the trainer . . . oh my. He is just the best I've ever been with. Ever!"

"Well, that's saying a lot," said Josie, elbowing her. Gabriela just nudged her back.

"What about *you*, Josie?" I asked. "You're always so quiet about your extracurricular activities."

"I'm a career girl most the time," she said. "But there is someone . . ."

"Oh yeah?" I said, raising my eyebrows. "Who?"

Josie leaned forward. "She's my producer at the station. We can't tell anyone. But I won't lie, it's pretty intense. I didn't even know I was into women until she came along. And it's not that I'm *exclusively* into women or anything . . . but I'm exclusively into her. We'll see what happens. I was . . . I don't know. I was afraid to tell you about her."

"Josie, that's amazing!" I said. "Why would you be afraid to tell us? I'm so excited for you!"

"Wow!" Gabriela said, clapping. "I love it! Josie, that's really terrific!"

"It's pretty new, but yeah. We'll see. So," Josie said, turning back to me, "you think Mr. Hebrew School is just a rebound thing, or is he going to stick around for a while?"

"Who knows?" I said. "But I feel like I've been on the rebound for seventeen years."

# SATURDAY

# Thirty-Eight

I stuffed my feet into my white fluffy slippers. It was time for the morning shuffle downstairs to make coffee, but without the weekday drop-off pressure. I refused to enroll my kids in endless weekend activities like sports teams that had you traveling to other states. Family time and our sanity meant more to me than team trophies. A controversial choice, perhaps, but it worked for our family. As I padded down the stairs, I wondered: Would Josh be up yet? Should I wake him? How would this whole thing work?

"She's up!" Josh called from between the stovetop and the sink. He was already in the kitchen with the kids, who were actually awake before me. Somehow he'd made them all chocolate chip pancakes (Zoe had apparently spared him the morning health-food lecture), and he was busy washing the pan while Max and Zoe ate. There wasn't a cellphone in sight as the three of them laughed and chitchatted.

Weren't the kids upset about their dad after what they'd learned about him? How was everything so normal? Families didn't just transform like this overnight. Maybe I shouldn't trust Josh. Maybe he wanted something from me. Maybe it was too good to be true?

But as Dayenu rubbed his adorable puppy face on my legs, I had to admit that this could all be a very positive development.

"If it isn't the worldwide sensation, Ella Rankin!" Max called out. "No, I mean Pippa Jones!"

"Funny, Max." I kissed him on top of his head. "So you finally got those pancakes."

"Mmm," he said. "So good!" He gave a thumbs-up sign.

"Mmm—*mmm*," Zoe mumbled, also giving her endorsement.

"Enough protein for you, Zo?" I asked.

"Actually, they're protein pancakes," Josh said.

"Of course they are," I said.

"So what's on the docket today?" he asked.

"Well, kids, what do you feel like? Josie and Gabriela are still asleep, right? To be honest, I was hoping to do a little writing this morning. I had a good idea last night."

"Can we go to that rock-climbing gym?" Max asked.

Zoe nodded, blasé. "That could be cool."

"I'd love to take them," Josh said. "Dayenu and I are excited for a drive today, aren't we?"

Dayenu raised his front legs, dancing a little to say yes.

"Seriously?" I said.

"Seriously. I'll drop them off and you enjoy time with your girl-friends. Yesterday was quite a day—it's the least I can do. And I'll be out of your hair. I've got classes all day, so don't worry about me."

Oh right. Teaching. School. Regular life. Suddenly I had a *lot* to write about.

I sat down at my desk and didn't even check email. I just opened a new document.

The cursor and I gave each other a hard look. But this time I won. The words came flowing out.

*Pain Points*

*By Pippa Jones*

*Life doesn't usually fall apart dramatically like in the movies with montage clips and boxes being packed*

228

*and decisions made on the spot. Life falls apart slowly. It drips and sags like a balloon deflating, air escaping no matter what you try to do. It circles the drain and causes pain in everyday moments, loading the dishwasher suddenly as sharp as a stab wound. It falls apart in glances. The empty master bed. Passports snuggled up together in a drawer. Family albums. All of it dissipated.*

*Loss is not just what's gone in the present but all of the future plans. The trips booked. The imagined graduation events. The holidays not celebrated together. Life falls apart in shudders, in emails from lawyers, drained bank accounts, trips to the ATM, new forms to fill out at the pediatrician, new boxes to check. Life falls apart in music stations no longer listened to, restaurants not gone to, food no longer eaten, dishes not ordered. Habits. Clothes. Preferences. Washed away.*

*The race of life shifts off balance and collapses, the race suddenly over, one runner alone in the field wondering what happened. Life falls apart in concert tickets not redeemed, in-laws that become distant, love evaporating everywhere.*

*Life falls apart in the shattered glass of what you thought would happen, who you thought would love you, who would be there as you made parenting decisions. In death, there is no choice. In divorce and deception, it's all preventable. And yet, it isn't. Abandonment. Unavailable answers. We don't choose these.*

*Life falls apart slowly. And just as slowly, we piece it
together again. One itty bit at a time. Steps forward.
Names changed. New loves discovered. New homes
built. Slowly, unsteadily, shakily, and yet, eventually,
solidly rebuilt.*

Okay, yes, it was a little heavy-handed, but it was done. An essay.
Beginning, middle, and end. It was evidence of my writing. And it was
good enough to sell. Somewhere. I was back in the groove. I could do
this. All of it.

I rewarded myself with a quick dip into my inbox.

One of the first emails said: "Hi Pippa! Congrats on *Blank*. I'd love
for you to be a guest on my podcast *Under the Hardcovers*. Any interest?"

Wait.

Stop.

I clicked on the Instagram link in the note and gasped. Rainbow-
colored shelves. Rippling abs. Twinkling eyes. Perfect skin. Aquiline
nose. Wavy hair. Yes! It was the hot podcaster that Gabriela originally
wanted me to set her up with. The one who inspired *Podlusters*. The
timing!

Maybe Gabriela would finally meet her match.

# SEVERAL MONTHS
# LATER

# Thirty-Nine

"Mom, is Dad coming to my bar mitzvah?"

I was sitting at my desk, dealing with my "Kids—VERY IMPORTANT" email folder, which had been languishing under all the other urgent folders. Camp forms, doctor's appointments, all the administrative things I'd been meaning to get to. As long as the emails were out of my inbox, it was almost as if I'd taken care of them already. And yet . . . no.

Max was standing in the doorframe, Dayenu right behind him, wagging his tail against the molding with a rather comforting thwack, thwack.

"What do you think, love?" I responded, spinning around to face him.

"No?"

"I think it's up to you."

Ethan had been dealing with legal issues since our driveway debacle. As it turns out, cheating on your spouse and paying a friend for sex weren't imprisonable offenses unless someone formally pressed charges. Which I hadn't. Yet.

Ethan had absconded to his brother's latest hotel property on Maui to wait out the storm and deal with the divorce papers I'd served him. Did he mind being away from the kids? He never mentioned it in the many emails he'd sent pertaining to our divorce. That hurt almost more than anything. Why didn't Ethan want to be involved with them? Did he truly not care? I couldn't stomach the thought.

But Max's bar mitzvah was a major life event. Surely he'd want to be there.

"I can email him and find out," I said.

I'd turned around to start the message when I heard Max say softly, "He probably doesn't even want to come."

I stood up from my desk and opened my arms to him.

"Oh, love," I said. "Of course he does. He's just going through a lot right now."

Max had finally mastered his haftorah portion—a good teacher could do wonders. I'd changed the plans from a temple reception immediately following the ceremony to a lunch for family only at the diner in the Beverly Hills Hotel basement. Max *really* loved their pancakes.

Small, simple, meaningful. No printed invites. No gift bags or photo booths. No frills.

"I wish I could make your dad behave differently," I said, looking Max in the eye. "You know that, right?"

"Yeah, Mom. I know," he said. "At least you're pretty cool."

"*Pretty* cool? How about, like, *unbelievably* cool?!"

He chuckled. "Don't get carried away."

"And despite his flaws, I know your dad loves you. Hey, can you take Dayenu out? It's been a few hours . . ."

"Sure. Come on, let's go, Dayenu!" he said. The dog jumped up and raced after him.

I shot off an email to Ethan, cc'ing our lawyers, asking if he planned to attend.

He quickly wrote back: "Yes."

Ah. Verbose.

I sent him a calendar invite with the details.

As the big day approached, the house filled with the sounds of Hebrew chants. Despite how secular our lives were, the sounds of Max and Josh reciting the ancient prayers to plucked guitar strings stirred my heart. There was something so essential, so fundamental, to it, all the generations of boys treading over the same letters and notes, ritualizing their transition to manhood. It felt like home.

When the big day came, Ethan *did* show up. And he brought a date who played Amal to his George Clooney. I couldn't miss them as they veered straight toward me. Suddenly, my navy A-line cap-sleeve dress and strappy heels seemed matronly compared to his date's sleek red pantsuit and stilettos. Not to mention that she was probably seven feet tall.

"Ethan," I said, nodding.

"Hi, Pips," he said, stopping in front of me.

"What do you think? Have you lost your 'Pips' privileges?" *Kidding, not kidding.*

He held up his hands and said, "Understood." If I couldn't joke, I didn't know how to handle the awkwardness.

I extended my hand up to the stunning mystery woman who towered over me. "Hi, nice to meet you. I'm Pippa."

"Leyla," she said in a sweet and sultry voice. "I've heard a lot about you."

"Yeah, I'll bet!" I chuckled. I could only imagine what Ethan had told her and how he'd spun my behavior over the past two decades. To him, everything was always my fault.

Wow, had it been six months since I'd seen Ethan? And in all that time, he hadn't seen the kids once. I honestly couldn't believe it. I missed the kids when they hung out with their friends for a couple hours. How could he go that long? I scanned Ethan's appearance like I was running him through the grocery checkout at King Kullen, every item beeping. Hair: less. Gray: more. Wrinkles: there. Belly: bigger. Beep!

"Leyla, why don't you sit up there, babe?" Ethan pointed to a row just up ahead as she smiled and sauntered off. *Babe?* Blech. Of course, she looked just as perfect from behind as we both watched her walk down the aisle. Bitch.

"Leyla seems really nice," I offered.

Ethan nodded, adjusting his tie and clearing his throat. "Yep. She's great."

"Wonderful," I said. "Let me know when she's old enough to get her driver's license."

"I see you haven't lost your way with words."

"Or yours with snark."

Just then, Max walked over in his navy suit, light-blue button-down, and simple striped tie and interjected. "Mom, Dad. Let's simmer down, okay?"

Max had grown up a lot in the intervening time, both physically—so much taller!—and emotionally. He was more assertive and even more self-possessed.

"Oh, we're not fighting," I said as Ethan extended his hand to shake Max's like they were business colleagues. "This is how we talk."

"She's right. Max?" Ethan said, hand still outstretched.

Max rolled his eyes. "I'm not going to *shake your hand*, Dad," he said. "Just . . . whatever. Enjoy the ceremony. Glad you could fit it into your busy schedule."

I motioned to Leyla and turned back to Ethan. "You going to introduce her?"

Max turned and looked. "Oh great. Just great. We didn't even invite you with a plus one!" And he stomped off.

"This is going well," I said. "So glad you came. And, you know, you should've been with someone like Leyla all along. I kept telling you that."

"I thought you were kidding," he responded. "Oh look, Zoe."

Ethan headed over to Zoe, who was sitting next to Josh. I could see her try to brush Ethan off as well. But, of course, I had to eavesdrop.

"So proud of Max," Ethan said to her. "Aren't you? This is a big day!"

Zoe looked at him and said, "Yeah, Dad. But they're *all* big. Glad you could make it to this one, at least." She had no plans to forgive her father.

I tried to hide my smile, impressed by Zoe's ability to stick up for herself, something I'd struggled with until recently. Josh covertly caught my eye and gave me a thumbs-up. In just a few months, Josh had become so much more to all of us than a tutor and friend. He had stepped into the void and filled it to overflowing. He'd become the partner who actually appreciated me. The constant who supported my kids.

We'd gotten engaged just before the bar mitzvah. His proposal was amazing. I'd been in touch with Derek Johnson (aka Black Jacket Guy) to accept his offer of LA Rams tickets. When we went (they were playing the Giants), Josh and I sat with the players' wives in a booth, the best view in the house. The crowds cheered at every down and went crazy for the series of touchdowns on both sides. I mostly ate popcorn and snuggled against Josh. Right before the fourth quarter, a video camera zoomed in on us.

"Wave!" Josh said.

"What the . . ." I exclaimed, as I smiled and waved and saw us on the Jumbotron.

Then, in front of everyone, Josh stood up, turned around to me, and got down on one knee. "Pippa Jones, will you marry me?!"

"Awww! Do it, girlfriend!" one of the wives called out.

"Say yes, mama!" another added.

"Go for it!" a player's son piped up.

The stadium erupted into a chant: "Do it! Do it! Do it!"

"YES!" I said, laughing. "Of course. Yes!" Not only were we on the Jumbotron, but we also made it on TV, which was an extremely efficient way to let everyone in the world know about it without having to send a single text or email. Highly recommend. Zoe and Max called my cell as soon as Josh slid a gorgeous round solitaire diamond on my finger.

"Josh told us to watch," Zoe said. "Mom, this is huge. Congratulations!"

"Mom! Josh! I'm so excited for you!" Max said.

*How was this my life?*

"We'll be home soon to celebrate," Josh added.

When the game ended, Derek had Josh and me come down onto the field to get our pictures taken with the whole team. If only I'd been a football fan, it would've been even cooler, but Josh was eating it up.

We got home to a house entirely filled with balloons. Even my mom and Seymour showed up for a quick congratulatory drink before rushing off to a canasta tournament.

Would it be happily ever after this time? Was that even still a thing? I had to believe it was.

# Forty

At the bar mitzvah, I sat on the bimah next to the rabbi, with Ethan on his other side. Zoe and Max were on the far side of the podium, thumb wrestling. When it came time for his part of the program, Max stood up, tugged at the bottom of his jacket, pulled his hair behind his ear, then looked at me and winked before striding confidently to the podium.

"*Baruch atah . . .*"

He read his Torah portion in perfect Hebrew. I was . . . kvelling. Meanwhile, what did it say about me that my favorite part of every Jewish service was the blessing for the bereaved? *Yisgadal . . .*

My mother and Seymour sat in the front row. Ethan's mom, Lisa, was on the other aisle, although she'd forgotten her hearing aid and continually asked, "What? What'd he say?!"

The podcaster, Scott from *Under the Hardcovers*, was there, too. Gabriela and I had zipped up to his West Hollywood studio as soon as he invited me onto his show. In a small-world moment, it turned out that his husband—yes, *husband* (so much for him being Gabriela's new love interest)—had been the editor of our college newspaper, the same editor who was so mean to us at Bluestone. With that behind us, we'd all hit it off and become fast friends. Even Josh thought Scott was a total mensch.

At the end of the beautiful service, Max stood up again, straightened his new tie, brushed his long hair out of his face, pulled his speech from his pocket, and resumed his place at the microphone.

He cleared his throat as he smoothed out the papers in front of him. I could only see his profile as he looked out at the audience—our extended family and other congregants attending the Saturday-morning service. Notably absent was Nathan, the menacing reporter. He'd been expelled from the temple despite his generous annual gifts. That had created a *lot* of discussion among the board members.

"Good morning," Max began. "As I thought about this speech, well, I kept trying to find ways to get out of it. Maybe I could find a prewritten talk on Google or ChatGPT?"

The crowd tittered. I shook my head, smiling.

"But if I've learned anything over the past few months, it's the importance of honesty and speaking from the heart.

"Becoming a bar mitzvah is about becoming a man. I now know what kind of man I want to be when I grow up. The kind of man I'm already starting to become. I also know the kind of man I *don't* want to be."

Max glared at Ethan, who coughed nervously and looked down at his lap.

"For one thing, I'm going to help more around the house."

Chuckles.

"And I'm going to learn how to operate every electronic device. But what I'm really going to do is remember to be there for the people I love. Being a man to me means being a sensitive and kind leader; helping everyone in my family; achieving my potential at whatever professional endeavor I choose; treating everyone, women in particular, with enormous respect; and never taking things for granted.

"Being a man means helping my community, giving back, and making positive changes. It means being a steward, passing along the faith and traditions to my own children. Being a man to me means tolerance, strength, love, and sacrifice. I've learned a lot from my family, the good and the bad. The real gift of my bar mitzvah is learning what kind of man I need to be—and how to become a mensch.

"So thank you. Thank you to everyone who showed me what I do—and don't—want to be like. Thank you to my mom for teaching me good values. Thank you to Josh for all the tutoring and for taking good care of my mom, Zoe, and me. Speaking of Zoe, thanks for the cellphone chargers. Thanks to my dad, for teaching me the difference between right and wrong—not *exactly* in the way I would've chosen. Oh, and also thanks to my mom, for showing me how to write my own story. Priceless."

My eyes brimmed with tears, and I smiled at my little guy, all grown up. All those nights of sitting outside his room until he fell asleep. All the sports classes I drove him to and then sat on the sidelines for, watching him shine. All the diapers changed, lullabies sung, forms filled out, and board games played. The towers built. The sheets tucked in. The shades pulled down. The shirts folded. The breakfasts made (well, microwaved). And here he was—thanking me. I hadn't done any of it with expectations. Mothering is just what I did from the heart, from the soul. It's who I was and who I am. And yet as all those moments with him flashed in front of me like an Instagram reel, it took everything I had not to weep.

Then Max smiled at me and the tears started flowing.

"I knew I could make her cry," he said, grinning. "In a good way!"

When his speech ended, Max came over and gave me a hug on the bimah. I didn't want to let go. Look at who he had become! As he sat back down in his seat, Zoe put her arm around his shoulders, and the two of them touched heads, smiling.

I couldn't have written it better myself.

# Forty-One

"Welcome, Pippa!"

It was publication day for *Blank*. Kevin and Cindy from *Good Morning, Coffee Lovers, with Kevin and Cindy!* had invited me back to their show, live and in studio. I was trying not to sweat. *Please don't have a flash now,* I prayed.

"Yes, Pippa, welcome back!" Cindy added. "We loved having you on for *Poppies*, and now you're back again with your latest: *Blank*!"

"That's right, Cindy," I said. "And actually, if it weren't for you and Kevin, I never would've written *Blank*."

"No!" they both said, feigning shock even though we'd rehearsed this before the show. Well, I hadn't prepped them on *everything* I was going to say.

"Yes! I watched you two break the news about Ella Rankin's last book, *Podlusters*, which had the same exact plot and name as the book I'd been writing at the time. I was almost two hundred pages in. I was devastated! I had to throw the whole draft away."

"Now that's gotta hurt," Kevin said, shaking his head.

"Oooh, rough!" Cindy echoed.

"It sure did. I couldn't write for months. I spent every workday sitting at my desk, staring at the cursor on the blank screen. I was totally blocked. The only thing that hurt more than that was when I found out my former best friend had *leaked* the idea to Ella."

"No!"

"Yes," I said. "And then I found her having sex with my husband."

Silence. The cameraman let out a chuckle.

I continued as Cindy, looking quite upset, made a cutting gesture to someone behind the camera.

"Cindy, I know you don't want me airing my dirty laundry. But I really want *other* families out there to know that not everything is perfect or easy. You never know what's going on behind closed doors. And it's not always easy writing books. Sometimes your entire first draft ends up in the trash and all you have is the blank page, a blinking cursor, and a deadline. And sometimes your best friend betrays you. But the important thing is to keep writing. Keep showing up for your friends. And keep prioritizing your family. The rest will all fall into place."

Before the broadcast could cut to commercial, Cindy put a hand to her earpiece. "Well, everyone. Looks like we have a special guest!"

"Ella . . . Rankin!" Kevin said.

"Hi, doll," Ella said, walking over to me, her full skirt swishing. "Hi, fans!" she said to the camera.

I kissed her on the cheek as we smiled. "Hi, El. Nice surprise!"

Ella had ended up buying the home down the street from me where we first met. She was a regular at our dinner table.

"You know, I was listening backstage," she said as she sat down, "and I really think you said something that people out there needed to hear, Pippa. I know I loved it."

The show's ratings that day skyrocketed; clips were posted and reposted all over TikTok and YouTube. Cindy and Kevin's producer said I had an open invitation to come back. And *Blank* went flying up the charts. Turns out, people really were craving the space to make a statement, and to tell their own stories. After all, stories are best when shared. Some people bought *Blank* to write in, others to draw in, some to collage. One reader turned the entire book into an origami Pippa. Readers were swapping their *Blank* books. *How do you fill in your Blank?* became a meme.

My wordless book stayed at #1 on the bestseller list for thirty-seven weeks. But who was counting? It was just long enough for me to write my next one, a novel about a middle-aged woman who found her calling.

Practices changed in publishing. Bookstores stopped accepting payments for better placements. Publishers gave every book a fair shot, letting the *readers* decide which ones really resonated with them. Many more book clubs popped up, so a few people's recommendations didn't control everyone else's behavior.

Best of all, readers connected. Pop-up cafés for specific books launched around the country, with individual Facebook groups uniting fans by title. Readers met each other at retreats and the salon of one particular book-fluencer I partnered with. The quantity shipped wasn't used to signal how important a book was to a publisher. Advance copies stopped being printed. The walls came tumbling down, and the publishing process itself became transparent, allowing for innovation of the system. The playing field was level for authors of all types to break in and tell their stories. And boy, did the stories come pouring in, connecting readers even more.

Some said *Blank* made the world feel a little bit smaller.

Somehow I'd started a movement.

# Epilogue

"Mom, look. See how he's looking at her?"

"Oh god," I groaned, pulling the covers over my head. "This again?"

"Yes! This is serious."

Zoe stood over me with the phone two inches from my face. Who needed a bedside light with that kind of illumination?!

It was the middle of the night. My National Book Award trophy sat on my bedside table next to my reading glasses. It didn't compare to Josie's Pulitzer for uncovering corruption in the publishing industry, but it worked for me. Michael had lost his position at Driftwood and gone into hospitality, managing a resort called the White Orchid. Still, his backing of my idea for *Blank* was life-changing. The ponytail girls were also fired from Driftwood when it came to light how much they'd enabled Michael's abuse. They were rumored to be starting a hair-care line called Pony Up.

My editor, Sidonie, was promoted into Michael's job by the board of trustees. Turns out Driftwood was ready for a woman to be in charge, and her success with *Blank* made her the perfect fit. My publicist, Brittany, was also promoted. She even hired a few of my LA author friends to build out her team: Maeve, Ada, Jane, and Will. They were all excited to make Driftwood into something new and innovative.

Kelly, who had ended things with Ethan to try to reconcile with her husband, Arthur, moved where she could more easily visit him in prison. Kelly and Arthur stayed together (with a lot of counseling) after he served his time. Gabriela, Josie, and I cut all ties with Kelly. Last I heard, she'd opened up a few tae kwon do training centers. She never published a book again.

Even with sales of *Blank* brisk right out of the gate, I still pursued my open-house strategy, which I'd thought was going to be the genius marketing idea for the book. I'd made little postcards about *Blank* and left stacks at every open house in LA—on people's desks, on their fridges, in their mailboxes, by their toilets. In some homes, I left the whole book. It was the very definition of a homegrown marketing campaign. It certainly generated buzz, so when @openhousebandit finally posted a few pictures, all it did was further propel sales.

"Zoe, I'll look," Josh said, sitting up in bed.

Josh and I had gotten married in our backyard six weeks after my divorce from Ethan was finalized. Of course Max and Zoe were our best man and maid of honor. Ella Rankin did a reading at the ceremony, and when she published her next book, *Stolen Goods*, she dedicated it to me. We'd had a blast when she had me on her podcast, *Subtext*, to discuss *Blank*.

I put my glasses on to look at Zoe's phone. It was a group of her classmates at Sevenford, in Northern California.

"Do you see how Taylor is looking at Ava? Do you think he's cheating on me?" she asked.

"Hmm," Josh said, studying the photo closely.

"Honey," I said. "I think that one day you'll find a love big enough that you won't need to analyze Instagram photos. That's what I think."

Zoe sat down on the edge of the bed.

"Like you guys?" she said. "I *wish*."

"Like us," I said. "Wait, I thought we weren't supposed to say 'guys.'"

"Whatever, I'm over it."

"Look," I said, "our relationship isn't *always* perfect—"

"Hey!" Josh interjected.

"Sorry," I said, kissing him on the cheek. "But, Zoe, it's the real deal. Marriage is a mix. Some days are warm, easy, loving. Other days you want to strangle the person because they've taken five minutes too long in the shower. But at the base of it all is trust, respect, affection, kindness.

"The real trick is being with someone who brings out the best in you, who sees you—well, *not* in the way my old boss, Michael, saw me; that's a story for another time—and makes you the best version of yourself. Someone who makes you feel safe so you can take risks, explore new places, conquer new challenges. That's what's important. And that's not anything you can find in a social media post."

"Well, maybe on Hinge," said Zoe.

"Zoe! My advice? Get off Instagram for your dating needs, get out in the world, make connections, find out what you like and who you want . . . and for the love of God, stop waking me up."

"Why'd you have to bring God into this?" Josh said with a playful grin.

"You make it sound so easy," Zoe said, "like this perfect relationship is just *out there* waiting for me."

"Honey, it *is*. You just have to know what you're looking for and who *you* are. And you have to believe you're going to find the right one. It might take a lifetime, but your person is waiting. There are so many people all over the world! They might not be in your dorm or even in California, but if you keep an open mind, look everyone in the eye, smile, be kind, be open, and see who else is enjoying the things you love, you just might find the ones who count. And give yourself the respect to not let *anyone* take advantage of you. I learned that the hard way."

"Deep, Mom," Zoe said.

"Thanks. I thought so."

We smiled at each other.

"Ladies, can I add something?" Josh asked.

I smiled. "Okay."

"I'd say *don't settle*, Zoe. If you feel like you're being silenced or taken advantage of or abused or anything, press the escape hatch. And then call me so I can beat the person up. I think that for every asshole out there, there are ten nice people. Life is short. But if you're with the wrong person, boy, can it feel long."

"So true," I said.

"Look for kindness," Josh went on. "Search for those moments of connection where you feel like you've known someone forever even though you've just met them. And be patient."

"Thanks," Zoe said. "I mean, I'd prefer *not* to have to wait to find love until I'm in my forties."

"Hey, there are *plenty* of perks to forty-love," I said.

"Like what?"

"Well, you'll just have to wait and find out."

I pushed Zoe's hair behind her ear, cupped her cheek in my hand, and beamed at her. She might have been all grown up, but she'd always be my baby. "And, God willing, I'll be here to cheer when you finally find the one."

"Morbid, Mom. Of *course* you'll be here."

"Let's just appreciate every day we get together. And preferably during the day, not in the middle of the night."

"Amen," said Josh.

We both giggled as Zoe slid off the bed, the room dark again. She stopped in the doorway.

"Hey, Mom? When are you going to tell everyone that you're the open-house bandit?"

I sat up again.

"What? You *know*?"

"Of course I know," Zoe said. "You've been sharing your location with me on your phone for years."

"Seriously?"

"Seriously. It's in Settings. I can change it if you want."

"You knew this whole time and you kept it a secret?"

"Yep. Well, now I've told Josh."

"What kind of bandit are we talking about," Josh said, still lying down.

"Maybe you should be a real estate broker, Mom. Maybe your writing days are over."

"Over? My writing days are just beginning," I said. "I'm thinking of getting into young adult novels. Maybe even writing a screenplay after my next novel comes out. But I guess I could do both, like the broker who wrote that great book about finding a soulmate in Paris."

Zoe just shook her head. "Whatever. Night, guys."

"Night, love."

"Night, Zoe."

I rolled over to face Josh.

"Tell me honestly. Did you think *Blank* was a good idea?"

He hugged me into his chest.

"I think *you're* a good idea," he said as we snuggled.

"Maybe that's the secret," I thought. Maybe life *was* a little more out of my control than I liked to believe. Maybe things like writing or falling in love didn't always happen exactly when I wanted them to. But once I stopped trying so hard to force them, the universe delivered. And the moments I least expected became the best stories of all.

All I had to do was share them.

Now, if I could just come up with my *next* book idea . . . *dayenu*.

# ACKNOWLEDGMENTS . . . FROM PIPPA

As many of you know, this book was a labor of love. At times, it was mostly a labor. It took me SO LONG to figure out how to follow up *Poppies* with something that all you readers out there would like and that I would feel proud of. And, as you now know, it came with a lot of uncertainty, self-doubt, and punitive thoughts. I just could not write the book.

And yet I did.

Thank you to my son, Max, for giving me the fabulous idea of the blank book and kicking all this off. I never would have thought of it myself. Don't kids just have the best ideas ever?! If only the rest of us didn't lose our youthful, imaginative way of looking at the world. Max, you went through a *lot* over the last few years and came out stronger for it. I couldn't be prouder of you.

Zoe, thank you for letting me write about you and all your teenage angst. (And hi, Todd and Damien!) I know I fictionalized some of this, but thanks for letting me use our private lives to make a book. No tattoos, please.

Mom and Seymour, thanks for being there when I needed you. As it turns out, it isn't the *way* we show love but the fact that we do it at all that matters the most.

Ethan, wow. Thank you for giving me Max and Zoe. And Lisa, thanks for that original introduction. I'm glad we can all be happier now, having gone our separate ways.

(Wasn't that incredibly civil of me?)

Josie and Gaby, thanks for being my ride-or-die friends, and especially for being there when everything was falling apart.

Kelly, you tried to steal my ideas, but I think we've established that even you can't do that. And actually you gave me the best story of all.

Ella, my newest BFF and writer-in-arms: your friendship is one of the best things to have come out of the last few years.

To Kevin and Cindy, please have me back on!

To Michael, my former publisher at Driftwood, thanks for clarifying my values and showing me that power isn't everything. I see you, too.

To Sidonie, here's to women-led publishing companies.

To Brittany, let's keep this publicity machine going!

To LeeLee, looks like you should've stuck around.

To Josh . . . where to begin?

If you had just taught my son Hebrew, *dayenu.*

If you had just taught my son Hebrew and not helped me turn the worst day of my life into the best, *dayenu.*

If you had just turned the worst day of my life into the best and not brought my family together again, *dayenu.*

If you had just brought my family together again and not made me fall head over heels in love with you, *dayenu.*

If you had just made me fall head over heels in love with you and not shown my kids right from wrong, *dayenu.*

If you had just shown my kids right from wrong and not brought Dayenu into our lives, *dayenu.*

It would've been enough.

# ACKNOWLEDGMENTS . . . FROM ZIBBY

Clearly my character Pippa has become a real person in my mind. It's going to be hard to put her aside after spending so much time in her shoes. I feel like she's about to walk in the door. Who knows? Maybe her adventures have just begun.

First, thank you so much to my Little A editor, Carmen Johnson, for taking a chance on me with *Bookends* and now again with *Blank*. Carmen, your ability to sort my good ideas from the bad without any kind of judgment and to make everything I write a zillion times better makes us a great team. I try so hard to please you—and make you laugh—with every draft. Thanks for turning me into an actual novelist. I hope this book is what you had in mind!

Thanks to rest of the team at Little A and everyone behind the scenes who made this publication possible, from the cover designer and the copyeditor to the marketing team and editorial staff. I know—all too well!—what it takes to publish a book, and I am forever indebted to you for publishing mine.

Thanks to my literary agent, Joe Veltre, for believing in me when I first showed up at your office and tried to convince you that I could really write. I told you I could do it! Let's keep this streak going. What's next?!

Thanks to my own team at Zibby Media for standing beside me; giving me the time and space I needed to write, edit, and market this book; and being the best friends and coworkers around. Seriously. I couldn't write without knowing you all had everything covered.

Thanks to the Zibby Books authors for all the encouragement and the early reads, the crew at Zibby's Bookshop, all our Zibby Books advisors and ambassadors, and everyone who has helped professionally.

Thanks to my husband, Kyle. Kyle, you showed me how to love, live, and laugh and helped me finish this book. Your dedication, devotion, and creative synergy make our relationship truly amazing. I can't say enough great things; you definitely helped me find my voice—and myself—again. Love all. *Dayenu.*

Thanks to my four kids, who I don't like to publicly name, which might just be stupid. I love you all so much, and just like Pippa, I'd give up all of it, everything, to protect you and be with you and know that you are happy. You are all so incredibly special in your own ways, and I couldn't do *any* of this without you. Seriously. **You're everything to me.**

Thanks to Gagy and Papa Kal, who are no longer with us. They published my one and only short story collection when I was ten years old and encouraged me to be a writer. It has taken me until now, at age forty-seven, to publish a novel. But I got here.

Gagy, I look at the picture of you and me together in Palm Beach (after you told Kyle he would look "a helluva lot better" if he just shaved that beard) every single day. It sits on my desk, next to my computer, so I feel like you're beside me at every step. How I wish you could still be here to see me publish this book after asking me on every single phone call, "Are you writing anything, dear heart?" I wrote something.

Thanks to my other late grandparents for teaching me the values that made me who I am today and which I've passed down to my own children.

Thanks to my parents and stepparents: my mom and Howard; my dad and Christine. The enormous love and support you've shown me— and the gift to be able to pursue my dreams—is above and beyond. I promise: these characters are not any of you! I could go on and on about what fabulous role models you are, even how you're responsible for my passion for books after watching you read constantly.

Dad, your approval means everything to me. I just want to prove to you that I'm not sitting around eating bonbons! You've given me the most powerful role model of success, entrepreneurship, kindness, and family prioritization. Knowing you'll always take my calls means more than you could even know. Thank you for your generosity and for leading by example. You make me laugh, smile, think, and feel. I love you.

Mom, without your early encouragement, I wouldn't be here. Thanks for always propping me up; offering to read and edit whatever I write; supporting all of my endeavors; being there for the kids, Kyle, and me nonstop; and for instilling your "good Midwestern values" in Teddy and me. I love you.

Speaking of Teddy, thanks to my brother; his wife, Ellen; and their three amazing kids for being so wonderful and filling my heart with love. Hoping for another power outage so we can stay over again soon! Who knew your kids would end up being my decorating consultants at the bookstore and my new office?!

Thanks to my in-laws Bernard, Miriam, and Stefanie for stepping in and helping with everything, especially in the day-to-day, and for sharing Nya. Our time in Amsterdam for the wedding was beyond special.

Thanks to all my author friends, whom I absolutely adore; every single guest who has ever been on *Moms Don't Have Time to Read Books*; all my Instagram friends and followers; booksellers, librarians, book industry folks, and book roundup writers; anyone who is in a book club—especially Zibby's Book Club(!); and everyone in the community who has been cheering me on. Special thanks to the team at *GMA* for letting me write the roundups for years and for doing the cover reveal.

Thanks to my best friends, especially my college and high school crews, and all my old friends whom I love so very much and don't see enough. That night when I was honored at the Child Mind Institute, I realized that when it mattered, you would all show up for me. It made me cry then and continues to do so now.

Thanks to all the editors and agents who rejected everything else I tried to sell. They all brought me right here, even if I couldn't see it then.

Mostly, thanks to you: the readers. Thank you for reading this book and for making all the time I spent typing, editing, thinking, imagining, refining, complaining, celebrating, strategizing, and stressing worth it. (Isn't writing fun?!) I sincerely hope you were entertained. Hopefully you also took something deeper away from it that just might help you in your own lives. Feel free to email me at zibby@bookendsmemoir.com if you loved the book. I read every email. Seriously. Thank you for coming along for the ride. You can follow my new Instagram accounts @pippajonesauthor, @underthehardcovers_, and @openhousebandit for more.

If you enjoyed the book, please review it on Amazon and Goodreads, post about it on social media, choose it for your book club, tell your friends, and spread the word! Yes, I'd love to come to your bookstore, event, festival, book club, or anything if I can make it work with my schedule.

Finally, thank you to the fictitious Pippa, Zoe, and Max, for allowing me to tell your story. Pippa, I hope you and Josh are happy, off in the land of characters written, lost but now found. Searching, just like the rest of us, for what it all means.

Thank you, everyone. I hope we meet again.

# ABOUT THE AUTHOR

*Photo © Sherri Puzey*

Zibby Owens is the author of *Bookends: A Memoir of Love, Loss, and Literature* and the children's book *Princess Charming* and is the editor of two anthologies: *Moms Don't Have Time to Have Kids: A Timeless Anthology* and *Moms Don't Have Time To: A Quarantine Anthology*. Creator and host of the award-winning daily podcast *Moms Don't Have Time to Read Books*, Zibby is the founder and CEO of Zibby Media, dubbed "the Zibby-verse" by the *Los Angeles Times*. It includes publishing house Zibby Books, online magazine *Zibby Mag*, Zibby's Book Club, retreats, classes, and events. She also owns Zibby's Bookshop, an independent bookstore in Santa Monica, California. A regular contributor to *Good Morning America* and other outlets, she loves recommending books as "NYC's Most Powerful Book-fluencer" (Vulture). A graduate of Yale University and Harvard Business School, Zibby currently lives in New York (with frequent visits to LA) with her husband, Kyle Owens of Morning Moon Productions, and her four children ages nine to sixteen. Follow her on Instagram @zibbyowens and on Substack, where she tells it like it is.